Augusta Webster

The sentence

A drama

Augusta Webster

The sentence
A drama

ISBN/EAN: 9783337303761

Printed in Europe, USA, Canada, Australia, Japan

Cover: Foto ©Andreas Hilbeck / pixelio.de

More available books at **www.hansebooks.com**

E SENTENCE

A DRAMA

BY

AUGUSTA WEBSTER

𝕷𝖔𝖓𝖉𝖔𝖓

T. FISHER UNWIN

26 PATERNOSTER SQUARE

MDCCCLXXXVII

DRAMATIS PERSONÆ.

CAIUS CÆSAR (Caligula), *Emperor of Rome.*
NUMERIUS AFRANIUS STELLIO, *A Roman knight.*
PUBLIUS CÆCILIUS NIGER, *Uncle to Stellio.*
QUINTUS LÆLIUS,⎫
MARCUS LÆLIUS, ⎭ *Brothers to Stellio's wife.*
MEMNON, *A Freedman of Caius Cæsar's.*
EUTHYMUS, *A slave of Stellio's.*
STEWARD *to Æonia.*
A BOY, *Son of Stellio and Lælia.*
LÆLIA, *Wife of Stellio.*
ÆMILIA, *Mother to Lælia : a widow.*
ÆONIA, *A Roman lady ; a widow.*
FONTEIA, *A Roman lady.*
NEDA, *A Freedwoman of Æonia's.*
LYDIA, *A slave of Æonia's.*
DULCE, *A slave of Lælia's.*
A GIRL, *Daughter of Stellio and Lælia.*

Guests ; Fisher-folk ; Peasants ; Mime-dancers ; Servants ; Roman Townsfolk ; Musicians ; Priests ; Youths *and* Maidens ; Lictors ; Soldiers ; Officers of State *and* others *in attendance on the Emperor.*

THE SENTENCE.

ACT I.

<small>SCENE</small> I. *Stellio's house in Rome: a spacious inner hall (peristyle)
with flowers and shrubs growing, and a fountain.*

<small>LÆLIA</small> *and* <small>CAIUS</small>, *talking in careless attitudes.*

Cai. 'Tis good to have stolen this sweet while of rest.
None in the world has soothed me ever like thee.

Læl. I'm glad I've soothed thee.   Yet it was unmeant,
Since nought knew I 'twas needed.

Cai.   And that's why.
Thou hast soothed me by thy gently being thyself,
And letting my cares be.

Læl.   Yet tell thy cares.
Thy baby playmate shared thy boyish griefs :
Now she's a woman, trust her.

Cai.   And I would :
But I've no griefs, dear : Fortune's on my side.
Only 'tis harder work than some could deem
To govern perfectly.   I'm very weary.

Læl.   Caius, 'mid the praise I hear just that thing blamed.
They say thy toil's pushed to a feverish stress.

Cai.   They know not duty, nor authority....
Vast burdens that, the mightier their strain,
The more do they make force in him that bears them.
They do not say my task's above my powers?

Læl.   What task?   Being Emperor?   No, no: all love thee.

Cai.   They *shall* love; but yet fear me.   Aye, what task?
Only to guide the world.   Only, alone,
To plan mankind anew : for that's the need,
Since I will have my men that govern just,
My men whose lot's subservient dutiful ;
All laws right and obeyed ; all customs honest ;
And crimes forgotten, being impossible.
Much, is that?   Not too much for power likè mine :
And yet—Oh, Lælia, I have done so little !

Læl.   No; much, much, much.   But so few months our head,
And to have done so much !   Oh, I have heard.
Never Augustus tasked his hours like thee.
They say thou'llt have his wisdom with his years.

Cai.   And is that all they say?   Well, I'll still labour.
I had fierce moods in boyhood——

Læl.   Never, Caius.

Cai.   Some knew I had fierce moods ; and blemishes :
But I have crushed youth and its faults in me—
Ended them, by my will, in a great breath—
So to become Rome's strong beneficence.
Thou know'st that means Rome's drudgingest labourer ?

Læl. It means *Rome's darling heart*, if it means thee :
That's what the people called to thee at the games.

Cai. They love me : yes. Well, talk to me of the games.
Respite ! Oh, respite now from plans and toils !
Let's hush the very thought. Were the games fine?
I spared no cost. Too many deaths for thee, though.

Læl. I never like the deaths. But 'twas a sight !
And didst thou note the lovely lady with me ?

Cai. I saw a lady lovely and a fool :
For when that fellow's teeth took the victor's throat,
And the passion shook us through, and the other women,
Most of them, caught the frenzy and fierce joy,
The wild-cat in them roused, and leaped to their feet,
I heard thee shriek, and looked : thy face was hid ;
Thou couldst not bear it——Well, we know our Lælia—
But she gazed fixed, demurely, pleasureless.

Læl. 'Tis true she took no pleasure in it, nor can ;
She says she tires of watching strife for nought.

Cai. For nought, forsooth ! They bleed, and writhe, and
   die.
What would the woman more ?

Læl.   That's waste, she says ;
Men lost without a good, pain for no purpose.

Cai. Purpose? Enjoyment's purpose. We need games.

Læl. I know. I laugh at her.

Enter STELLIO *and* NIGER.

Stell.   Caius, all welcomes.

Nig.   Good greeting.

Cai.   Greet thee, Niger.   Stellio, thanks.
Thy Lælia makes me truant here too often.

Stell.   Often ; not once too often.

Nig.   Not too often.
Indeed, dear prince, trust old experience,
This early half-hour thieved from tasks too close
Makes the other half-hour's toil worth twice an hour.
Well, niece, who's she thou'llt laugh at ?

Læl.   'Tis Æonia :
Thou knowst she'd have no games.

Nig.   No games, no Rome.

Stell.   They have their use.   Valour and to endure,
These, seen in frequent shows, imbue our folk,
As the nurse's aimless talk teaches babes speech :
Even our women learn a Roman strength,
They can see blood and keep their nerves.

Cai.   Can Lælia ?

Stell.   I'm caught :   I had forgotten Lælia.

Læl.   Nay.
Not me ; only my fault.

Cai.   A pretty praise :
So he forgets thy faults, but never thee.
That's good.   And therefore I am much his friend.

Læl.   We know it.

Stell.   And much thank thee.

Cai.   Thank me not.
Not till I've made thee fortunate—Nor *me* then,

But this little wife by whose fond eyes I see thee.
Make her less pale and blushing, though.   She's changed.

   Læl.   I am older : can he help it ?

   Cai.   Would he could !

For if he could I'd make it death in him
If ever he changed thee from the child thou art.

   Læl.   Child ! I ! A five years' wife !

   Cai.   Is it so long?

And yet thou hast scarce more years, count all those five,
Than *my* wife when we married.

   Nig.   Would she had lived !

And the babe she should have borne thee !

   Læl.   Would indeed !

But now he'll wive. 'Tis time, and—Baby's crying ! [*Exit within.*

   Cai.   If all my soldiers, now, at the first blast,
Would hurry so as mothers to these trumpets !
But, wife and child for me, thou sayst, good friend ?
My widowhood, long my mere private fact,
Has since become Rome's loss.   I know my duty :
I shall take steps.   Æmilia seeks my spouse....
Some girl of Rome's chief houses, grave and gracious,
A woman fit for policy and for home,
Such as Æmilia's self in vigorous youth.

   Nig.   Then much unlike her daughter.

   Cai.   And that's true.

Daughter to mother never was less like
Than Lælia to Æmilia—save in honour :
And both sorts are too rare.   And, of both sorts,

I could love neither loverly; but love worse.
And so I choose what's fit—not I, Æmilia—
For first I'll be Rome's husband, then my wife's:
She'll count Rome part of me, our children Rome's,
And live for Rome in us.   What? [*looking at a dial*].   That
    the time !
I'm late again.   Hours need more minutes—scores. [*Exit.*

   Nig. He's worthy all Rome's love.   But would he'd
    slacken!
Pressed gallop always never won a race.
Nephew, what was't he said of Lœlia changed ?
Dost know that Lœlia's sad ?

   Stell.   She always smiles.

   Nig.   To thee.

   Stell.   I say not that.

   Nig.   No ; 'twere to boast.
The bride's pleased fondness from the accustomed wife,
That's a choice flattery of a man's deserts.
Eh, eh ?   Let's talk, my boy ; I'm old and love thee.
She hides her sadness ; that defines it real :
Some peak for whim, some to be bribed to smile,
But Lœlia—she's the sweetest soul in Rome.

   Stell.   She's a good, gentle creature.

   Nig.   And a lovely.

   Stell.   Few lovelier.

   Nig.   Not one.   Not one her match.

   Stell.   When thou wast young some ladies *had* a lover !
I'm sure thou swor'st them to the stars.

Nig.   Belike.

Belike I was a fool and she a fool,

If any she and I tit-tattled love.

However—Lælia, when thou'rt musing, gazes,

Hands loose on lap, and then she'll bite her mouth,

And ply her needle hastily like a task,

Then fetches thee her children, watches dog-like

For thy caressing them.

    Stell.   Well ; and what's her ill ?

    Nig. That's what I wonder.

    Stell.   I do all she asks,

Give lavishly, exact not, find no fault,

I'm tender to her. My wife has a good lot.

    Nig. 'Tis true. I say no other.

    Stell.   'Tis past bearing !

I am her husband, not a sweetheart boy,

She has had the fumes of nigh five amorous years,

And if I bate some trifle of the incense,

Or she so dream, must she play meek despair,

And show me for the tyrant that thou sayst ?

    Nig. Tut ! Tut ! I say no tyrants. Nephew, hark,

Although I prize the niece thou gav'st me high,

My care herein's for thee. Say that thou wrong her,

Well, women have a savouring joy in wrongs,

A pleasure in well pitying themselves ;

She's safe enough ; 'tis thy case needs regard.

Thy kin, both sides, match not, with all the hand,

A finger wagged by one of hers.

Stell.   Fool, I !

Who thought my high alliance should be strength !

Nig.   Why, so it is, and will be.

Stell.   Of what sort ?

Strength such as rivers give their confluent brooks.

I am not Stellio, find not my own road :

I am whelmed into the river where I'm part :

I am kinsman of the Lælii ... strong, and nothing.

Nig.   And her portion, if they take her back : thou'rt poor.

Stell.   Not poor enough to keep her for her portion.

Nig.   Well, well, that point's the least.   Myself could help.

Since my last died, thou'rt heir of all my sons :

My own dear sister's one dear son, all's thine.

Stell.   All my life long thou hast been my friend and father.

Nig.   Dear boy !   Third point, and chief——

Stell. [*interrupts*]   We still talk Lælia ?

Nig.   The third point's Caius friend to thee or foe.

I doubt young Caius will have no more loves,

As he loves Lælia still, impassionately,

Thus certainly, and so tender.   Lose not Lælia.

Stell.   She has the winds of favour in her hand ;

She'd waft my vessel into port : I know it.

Yet, Niger, there are women—Caius seeks one—

Could help a man to take from Fortune's hand

More and more worthy prizes than——Ah, well !

Lælia's a sweet kind wife.

Nig.   Yea, will she so ?

Some shrewder woman help thee more than Lælia ?

Thou'rt thoughtful now?

Stell.   Whether, as I had meant,

To wait more ripeness, or now speak.   Well, now.

Know I shall need thee my negotiator—

And Lælia's—with her kin.   She's sad, thou sayst :

That's that she'd be far happier quit of me.

We are no comrades.   One of liker sort,

A playfellow, gay, simple to content,

That's her right match.   And him has Lælia found.

Nig.   They lie who tell thee so.

Stell.   She thinks no ill.

But young Metellus cannot hide his hurt.

Nig.   She loves Metellus?

Stell.   What she would she knows not :

But that, once quit of me, she'd wed Metellus,

Is certain as that lambs will nibble grass ;

And I'll not block her way to fitter union.

Nig.   Divorce her?   Ruin thyself?

Stell.   I have thought all.

'Twould be my service to her, to her house,

My yielding her to the best match in Rome.

Nig.   The shrewder woman needs her place.

Stell.   What woman ?

Does Lælia say?

Nig.   How can she, saying nought ?

Stell.   But who's the other woman?   Give her name.

Nig.   I cannot.   And that's strange : since Lælia pined

I have somewhat watched thee.

Stell.   Aye ?

Nig.   And never a sign.

Stell.   And never a sign should be the sign of nought.
Tell me, could'st thou break this to Lælia's kin?

Nig.   If 'twere resolved.

Stell.   Or, rather, sound them first :
First sound Æmilia.   Lælia's mother won,
As a proud mother may be with such lure,
She'll soothe away her daughter's last regrets,
And give Metellus field.

Nig.   Tut !   Nephew, nephew !
This is to build on air.   What's thy scheme's base ?
Lælia desires Metellus : thou'llt consent ;
She'll ask her kin to thank thee for a service :—
That's sense.   But now thou hast talked it upside down :
Not she desires, but would her mother make her :
The superstructure is to found the base.
'Ware, or 'twill tilt, and batter thee into dust.
But what says Lælia ?   Hast thou parleyed with her?

Stell.   Not yet : save covertly last night.

Nig.   And then ?

Stell.   She scarce seemed startled : somewhat dazed.   She
    comes.

Re-enter LÆLIA.

Nig. [*aside to Stellio*] Stellio, the child has wept.

Læl.   How blue the heaven !
I thought 'twould rain.

Nig.　　　　　　There's rain been in thine eyes.
What brought it there?

Lal.　　　　　　There *must* be sometimes rain.
Now, why has Dulce moved my broidery loom?

Nig.　Come, let the broidery be.　Give me thy hand.
We'll help thee, child, believe it, I and Stellio.

Lal.　No, no!

Nig.　　　　　　How! wilt thou weep again for that?
Come, "No" to what?　For I had proffered nought.

Lal.　Then no to nought.

Nig.　　　　　　　Plain words: wilt wed Metellus?

Lal.　Husband!　Dost thou so hate me? [*Going.*]

Stell.　　　　　　Lælia, hear us. [*Exit Lælia.*

Nig.　Her heart's still in thy hand; and keep it—keep.
Be happy spouses.

Stell.　　　　　Would to God we could.　[*Going.*]

Nig.　Aye, follow her; soothe her. [*Exit Stellio*] *She* win o'er
　　her kin!
'Tis well I tried her.　But is Stellio crazed?
Nigh lose so sweet a wife, and she his fortune!
Not jealous either, not enraged, not—Nothing!
Well, I'll go buy a basket full of toys:
It brings her merry when the babies laugh.　　　　　　[*Exit.*

ACT I.

SCENE II. *The same.* LÆLIA *asleep.*

Voice without. Madam, she's here.

Enter ÆMILIA *and* DULCE.

Æmil.   What, dropped asleep? Stop, Dulce,
Awake her not: I'll wait. Go, my good girl. [*Exit Dulce.*
She sobs in sleep. Oh, what's her secret !

Læl. [*asleep*]   Husband !
Not that ! Not that !

Æmil.   And she still praises him !

Læl. [*asleep*] He has taken the children from me too !

Æmil.   Ill dreams.
I'll wake her. Lælia ! 'Tis not sleeping time.
Dear child, arouse thee.

Læl. Mother ! [*clings to Æmilia and weeps passionately.*]

Æmil.   Come, what's this?
Be still, be still, dear. What ! my singing-bird !
My little rose of the morning ! Mother's sunshine !
Oh, foolish sunshine, all in mist and tears !

Læl. No ; for the mists are gone now I'm well waked.
That's what all sunshine does.

Æmil.   Does it, my child?

I cannot much remember thee in tears.

Læl. Dear mother, no.   I have had happy homes :
At home, and here with Stellio.

Æmil.   Hast thou now ?

Læl. Yes, yes, indeed.   Oh, such a happy home !
Pray for me well that I may never lose it.

Æmil. How shouldst thou lose it ?

Læl.   If I died I should.

Æmil. Am I to pray that thou shalt never die ?

Læl. Oh, cross cross-questioner, measuring my poor words !
One needs must sometimes talk beyond the bounds.

Æmil. Look at me, daughter ; look me in the eyes.
Thou canst not.

Læl.   Wherefore not ?   I do no ill.

Æmil. And yet, behold thou canst not.

Læl.   Thou'rt unkind.

Æmil. Daughter, thou art a mother.   By and by,
When thou shalt see thy girl a woman too,
After the years while thou hast spent out all—
Thy hopes, thy strength, thy will, thy sap of life—
For her unconscious using, made, for years,
Her young light life thy consecrated end,
As guardian priestesses their deity,
Then, when time comes that she might pay her debt
With the mother's single price, her daughter's trust,
Tell me what should she do, thine own Afrania?

Læl. Chide not.   I love thee, mother.

Æmil.   Is it love,

Is it daughter's love, to hide thy sorrows from me?

Læl. Thou naughty mother, I must chide thee now.
Why dost thou, evil ominous, say sorrows?
Sorrows are carriers flying past the homes;
Call them by name 'tis there they'll come to perch.
We'll never name them. Hush! They are flown by,
I heard their whirring wings. Talk now of joys.

Æmil. Nay, nay, my trifler, thou'llt not slip me so.
To-day I know.

Læl.   Oh! tell me what.

Æmil.   Nought, nought.
I meant I've learned from thee: I've nought to tell.

Læl. See how thou hast frighted me. I thought, good sooth,
Thou hadst some strange bad tidings. Foolish me!
Come to the garden: there the children play.

Æmil. 'Tis Stellio keeps thee wan.

Læl.   Then 'tis of love.

Æmil. I and thy brothers made him; for our price,
Thy happiness. But if he cheat of that!—
I think he'd liefer please such creditors;
I think we have some potency.

Læl.   Harm not him!

Æmil. Nay, I'm thy Stellio's friend, his fosterer.

Læl. Thou best, kind, selfless, mother! But for thee—
A thousand times I say it and love thee new—
Save but for thee I had not been his wife.
They were so proud and foolish, all the rest,
As if some usual man, by usual greatness,

Could be worth more than Stellio, being he.
But thou couldst see.

Æmil.   Aye ; could I ?   There's my question.
Dear, tell me all.   Tell me I bid thee.

Enter QUINTUS *and* MARCUS.

Æmil.   Come.
Hover not at the entry : ye are needed.
All's true : your sister's foully used.   She owns it.

Læl. Oh, mother !

Æmil.   Owns it : for that grief we marked
She feigns away.   Would she, wer't natural ?
But she's afraid of Stellio.

Læl.   Say not that.

Quint.   If that be rightly guessed—

Læl.   Brother, he's kind.

Marc.   By all the gods, if that be rightly guessed,
We'll have her back ; then tear his sprouted wings,
Remake him worm, and crush him.

Quint.   Who's thy rival ?

Læl. In heaven's truth, I know of none.

Æmil.   Nor fear'st ?

Læl. No one ; oh, no one.   Let me swear it, no one.

Quint.   Since thou'rt so earnest, we believe thee, sister.

Marc.   More that such secrets, like rank scents through air,
Reek to all nostrils.   'Twould have reached us.   Yet—
Then, Lælia, what's thy ill ?

Quint.   Better ask Stellio.

Læl.   Misuse me not.   How dare you twit my husband?
I know you love me well ; therefore trust him.

Quint.   Well, well, we'll rest content.   But fool us not.
Thou dost so cherish him thou'dst bear shown slights ;
But we were shamed if we should bear them for thee.

Læl. Oh, Quintus !   And thy wife?

Marc.   She has thrust thee now]

Quint.   Oh, she may mock.   She knows that's other gear.
The Lælii's sister is—is not my wife.
My wife's content too, proud to be so wed,
Sure of my trust, at ease in my goodwill :
And, if she thinks when beauty flashes nigh
I scarce conceive a husband a man dead,
She thinks, on top of that, she's my home matron,
And friend of me who'd lose—aye that I would—
Ere part our wedded hand-clasp, twenty loves.

Læl.   Friend !   Matron !   Yet some husband's wife, silly
    soul,
Might liefer be, were it one of twenty loves.

Æmil.   Lælia, 'tis no right uttering, meant or mocked,
Which counts that confident and grave regard,
The leal wife's due, ev'n fickle husbands pay,
Less prize of womanhood than love's short zeals.
Nay, and I pity not good wives like his,
But more his twenty loves . . . their twenties too.
Oh, this sick satiate license of our Rome !
Love, and then jade, then love and jade, then—more of it ;
And chop and change their lovers, hands around.

Would 'twere no worse, not chop and change the spouses !

Marc. Aye, that reminds me : there's a new divorce ;
Licinius and Valeria break their marriage.

Æmil. And wherefore ?

Marc.   Mutual preference for release.
She takes her father's part with whom he has feud,
And he'd fain wed Æonia.

Quint.   What !

Marc.   No fear.
He's just as like to have the moon to wife :
Or thou to win thy wooing.

Æmil.   Who's Æonia ?

Lal. Not know !

Quint.   Ask that !

Marc.   Who !

Æmil.   'Tis no name.

Quint. Loveliest in Rome.

Lal.   My neighbour since last March ;
Widow of that rich knight they called The Boor.
He kept close house and cramped on the Viminal ;
She slipped the unworthy shell and found her fit,
Lollio's cast mansion that she bought. I'm glad.
She's chary of her neighbour visits, though.
And when we are together there's a something—
Her perfectness, her soft imperious calm—
Something that makes her more than I too much.

Æmil. I mind me now. A low-born loveliness :
Her father sold her wife to hoar Cominius

Above her rank ; he dead, she married higher.
Æonia—yes.   But sure they told me this,
By her unlikely natural quality,
She reared herself to such a reverend worth
As Rome's signorial wives in nobler days.
Were she still thus, though lowly for thy friend,
I would not, Lælia, say "frequent her not :"
But a slight beauty-dame for wooings—

Læl. ⎞
Quint. ⎬   No.
Marc. ⎠

Æmil.   Thine, Quintus.

Quint.   All my wooing was first word :
I doubt there's none will ever dare the second.

Marc.   Save whom she'll wed.   For me, I warn thee, mother,
If once my eyes caught on her marble smile
A softening quiver, I should woo her then—
Woo her, so worthy thee, to be thy daughter.

Æmil.   There are great ladies worthy ; even now,
Woo one of them.

Marc.   And so some day I will.
But our best pearls of beauty to Æonia
Are any loveliness to Helen's self.
Well, is all said with Lælia ?   Are we eased?

Læl.   How else ?   And, mother, come with me within ;
I need a housewife counsel.   Idlers, go.

Quint.   Oh, gracious hostess !

Marc.   And oh, gracious sister !

Læl.   Oh, gracious brothers, wasters of my time!

Yet, pray you, dears, soon waste me time again.   [*Exit within.*

Quint.   Mother, farewell till evening.

Marc.   I'll return;

I'll fetch thee, mother.

Æmil.   I'll not wait so long;

I shall be home ere thou.

Marc.   Till dinner then.

> [*Exeunt Marcus and Quintus.*
> [*Exit Æmilia within.*

ACT I.

SCENE III. *The same.*

Enter FONTEIA *and* DULCE.

Font. Thy mistress is not here.

Dulce.   I'll find her, Madam.

Font. Stay, my good Dulce ; prithee set this scarf.
Thou hast not bid me welcome back to Rome.

Dulce. I feared to be too bold, so did but think it.
Thou wast long away.

Font.   A life ! an age, my child !
I thank thee ; that's well folded. Yes— 'Tis well.
Prithee tell Lælia I am longing for her. [*Exit Dulce.*
I would I had that girl ; mine's clumsy-handed ;
She set this scarf ten times and each time worse.
Aye, now 'tis as I meant it, moulds the shape,
Yet has a veiling grace.

Voice without.   Madam, this way.

Enter ÆONIA.

Æon. Fonteia !

Font.   Lovely Æonia lovelier !

Æon. Welcome to Rome. I knew not thou'dst arrived.

Font. Since yester-eve. I'm on my way to tell thee :
But, passing, came here first. Thou'rt something changed ;
Thy face is—Nay, I know not what's the change.

    Æon. Belike there's none in only these six months.

    Font. Woe's me ! They seemed six years. Six months
      from Rome !
And, oh, my tedious husband all the while !

    Æon. Still feather-brained ?

    Font.   And thou, still leaden-hearted ?

    Æon. Why leaden ? *My* heart's been less weighty, sure,
Than *thine* that ever held some thoughts too much.

    Font. Leaden with lifelessness, weighty with pride.
But come, thy news.

    Æon.   I've none.

    Font.   That can ill be.
Thou hadst thy choice in Rome, when I went forth,
Of well-nigh every hand man had for wedding,
And well-nigh every heart man had for wooing :
Which is it, spouse or love, thou hast chosen ? Whom ?

    Æon. For spouse—I'll wait to find a man worth love :
And the other choice——I am the same Æonia.   [found.

    Font. Well, well. Then 'tis thy spouse worth love thou'st

    Æon. Is such soon found ? Thou hast forgotten me.

    Font. I know thou art ambitious.

    Æon.   Say I *was.*
But I'm scarce lowly now, and rich, and valued ;
And whither could I rise that, for a woman,
Is higher than loving proudly ?

Font.   Proudly : see.
Oh, but I know thee there.   Thy beauty's winged ;
 Twill float thee upwards still.

Æon.   I meant not that.

Font.   Indeed I know thee not then.   Times on times
Thou saidst Love, being blind, has ever a guide
That takes him where to grasp in the dark and hold—
As Vanity, Lightness, Pity, and all desires—
And Love could start no footstep for Æonia
If less than grave Ambition led the way.

Æon.   I have looked closer on the world, and seen.
To-day Ambition has no lure for Love.
Power in a man, rule, leadership of the crowd,
Aye, that belike would thrill a woman's heart,
Flush her hot pulse to the fire of very love,
And the man might be to her as—as, perchance,
One loved for his own sake.   But long ago—
Some woman and some man in the emulous days,
Before Rome strung all bits into one bridle
And passed the handling to her emperors.
In modern order, power's to run in harness,
A leader's foremost in a driven team,
Rule's to have leave to serve.   Pomp, honours, worship,
All signs of power, the great still have : power, no.

Font.   And yet these pomps and honours and poor signs,
Since they're our best, if thou be still Æonia,
Thy soul desires them.

Æon.   Surely ; or 'twere weak.

I do but say (if we *must* babble of love,

And if love be a better boon than these),

That—that love is love.

 Font.   Thou hast learned a wisdom.

 Æon. Aye ; fit to answer folly. Now let's talk.

How went thy journey?

 Font.   Prithee tell me who ?

Oh, Master Love has windows in thy face,

And sheds a sort of light there ; thou'rt betrayed :

So tell me all.

 Æon. Wait for the all to tell.

 Font. Cæcilius? No. Lentulus? Piso? No.

Longus ? Nay, thou'lt not stoop to him I'm sure.

Stay, Marcus Lælius—he's the best—'tis he.

 Æon. Prithee, Fonteia ! Will thy list not end ?

I like not this : I am not wont, thou know'st,

To be a theme for guesses of such sort—

One name, and then another, He ? or He ?

Name me no loves and spouses : I have none.

 Font. Oh prickles, prickles, prickles, to this rose !

" I can't be gathered ; no." And yet, the while,

Shears at the stem, and some one—I'll be dumb.

 Æon. Do, prithee, till thou find a better theme.

 Font. [*aside*]. 'Tis Marcus Lælius : and they fear Æmilia.

     Enter STELLIO.

 Stell. Æonia ! This is water to parched lips.

And I so needing counsel with thee now !
They told me 'twas Fonteia.

Æon.   She is here....
For whom (since I and thou, Stellio, I think,
Met few days since), thine ecstasy was framed.

Stell.   Pardon me, fair Fonteia, that my sight,
Eager to find thee, could not pierce that column ;
And take my welcome, now.   'Tis with my heart.

Font.   It is, if that be mine Æonia had.

Stell.   Still quaint and merry.   Nay, that was her own.
Her visits are so rare we, all here, greet them
As though like thee she came by sea and land.

Æon.   I doubt if Lælia knows we're here.

Stell.   She does.
At least she knows Fonteia honours her,
And sought to attend her : but her head so aches
She could not quit her pillow.

Font.   Ill, poor dear ?

Stell.   'Twill pass, she says, with sleep.   She sat in the sun.

Font.   Sleep's the best cure.   I'll come to her to-morrow.

Æon.   And now to *my* house.

Font.   Presently, if thou wilt.
Why should I run from Stellio ere we've talked ?

Stell.   That's kind, dear lady ; grant me some good minutes.

Font.   You'll hold that counsel though, you two, first while.

Æon.   I have none to hold.

Font.   I *have* then ; with these fishes.   [*withdraws
                                to the fountain*].

Font. [*aside.*] Is't possible? His ruin! The fall for her !
Yet he spoke confident. She went red and pale :
That might be solely wrath. Oh, she'll rebuff him.

Stell. I dare not speak : thou'rt ice.

Æon.   '   Have I not cause ?

Stell. 'Twas seeing thee suddenly whirled me off my guard.

Æon. Note, then, how well it is we rarely meet.

Stell. 'Tis wise : but well? Ah me !

Æon.   Follow Fonteia.
But—Lælia and Metellus? Will she ?

Stell.   No.
Not yet. Never, perchance. Hope blinded me.
'Twas named outright just now : I'm out of heart.

Æon. What said she ?

Stell.   She cried out : 'twas pitiful.
She has wept since, I know, and that's her headache.

Æon. Would I had burrowed where my husband left me !
Then had I been no Lælia's neighbour here,
And not have known thee, Stellio. All were well
If thou had'st still loved Lælia, knowing me not.

Stell. I *have* known *thee.*

Æon.   We venture talk too long.
[*calls*]. Fonteia, come and hear this jest.

Stell.   One moment.

Font [*calls*]. Jest on ; I'm busy.

Stell.   Let me touch thy hand.

Æon. No, no.

Stell.   Thou'rt pitiless wise. Then but stand still
Thou know'st not how I have hungered for thy face.

Enter Æmilia.

Æmil. [*aside*]. His gaze ! Her tremulous lips, drooped eyes !
  They're mute.
Too ominous signs.   And why has Fonteia left them ?
  Font. Æmilia ! Dearest Madam, I greet you well.
  Æmil. [*aside*]. They stood not close and yet, on the sudden
    start,
Moved more asunder : proof they feared suspicion.
Why should they, save they've secrets ? [*aloud*] Yes, Fonteia—
I mean good-day—oh, pardon me my slackness,
My mind was busy : all good welcomes home.
  Font. All reverent thanks, and loving.
  Æmil.   Good son Stellio,
Dost thou not tell me who is this fair dame ?
  Æon. One proud to greet the noble dame Æmilia ;
Æonia, Madam.
  Stell.   And our neighbour friend :
Whom thou'llt have known by Lælia's praise ere now,
Seeing she likens hers to thine own worth,
As Marcus does.
  Æmil.   I have heard of thee, Æonia.
I heard thy loveliness was no snake's skin,
As are too many, but the case fit wrought
Of honourable virtue.
  Æon.   That repute
I can dare claim, of honourable virtue,
And prize it my chief jewel.
  Æmil.   Worthily thought.

And yet 'tis not repute but virtue's self
That's our true jewel : fair repute's the setting.
Lose the true stone a mock can fill its place,
And shines a while ; but the cheat never wears.

   Æon.   And so the counterfeit much more abases
Than to have worn no jewel.

   Æmil.   Say'st thou so ?
'Tis a true word ; but proud. Thou'llt keep thy jewel,
If 'tis so true a diamond.

   Æon.   Madam, I shall.

   Æmil.   But, ladies, we talk standing.

   Font.   We must go.
Or I must—and Æonia was in haste.
Soon as we heard dear Lælia could not see us
She would have dragged me to her house to chide—
She always chides me—I for once was rebel :
'Twas Stellio's fault, who welcomed me too much :
We laughed so that I ran to the mute fish
To rest my ears.

   Stell.   Leaving poor me as mute.

   Æon.   Noble Æmilia, let me take my leave.

   Æmil.   Good day, fair madam ; 'twas good hap to meet thee.
[*aside*] Good hap, whichever way.

   Font.   I kiss thy hand.

   Æmil.   Good day, Fonteia, still the giddy pate ;
Gods make thee wise as merry.

   Font.   Good day, Stellio ;
Good day, my prince of welcomers.

Æon.   Good day, Stellio.

Stell.   Farewell, dear ladies ; honour us soon again.

                              [*Exeunt Æonia and Fonteia.*

Æmil.   Stellio, I'll think my Laelia fills thine eyes ;
But that's a dangerous beauty, gaze not on it.

Stell.   Æonia's is it !   Why ! she's past approach ;
In triple mail ; Medusa to all comers,
Looking them into stone for an idle word.

Æmil.   Then speak thou to her none.

Stell.   I !   Sooth I dare not.
I'd not dare wrong her so.

Æmil.   I'd fain have heard
" I would not so wrong Lælia."   But 'tis well.
Keep in that mind, my son.

Stell.   Of that be sure.
What, going ?   Shall I walk with thee to thy house ?

Æmil.   Aye, if thou wilt.   No ; tarry lest Lælia wake.
I doubt ye have quarrelled, for she wept a deal,
Then feigned some nothings for it.   Ease her heart.

Stell.   I'll pleasure her to my best.   She's fanciful.

Æmil.   Or *thou* art.   Well, good-bye.

Steil.   I'll find thy servants.

                              [*Exeunt Stellio and Æmilia.*

ACT I.

SCENE IV. *The same, in the evening.* LÆLIA *and* Handmaids *at work:* LÆLIA's two children *playing beside her:* DULCE *singing.*

SONG.

Pluck the rose part blown,
Fresh to-day ;
So it will not have been shown
That there is a pause to light,
That there is a chill in night,
So it will not feel decay.
Pluck the rose ere it have known,
As some roses may,
One soft petal shrink or stain or drop away.

Læl.   I love that song, my Dulce.

Boy.   I love drowsy.

Læl.   What's drowsy, pet ?

Boy.   She sang it : sing-song drowsy.

Dulce.   'Tis but a lullaby I sang him at noon.

Enter NIGER.

Nig.   Thou'rt quickly cured, sweet niece.   And what was ailing ?

3

Læl.   Only a heavy head.

Nig.   The weather's close.
Thou should'st breathe country freshness this hot summer.

Læl.   But Stellio finds our farm on the hills too dull.

Nig.   Then take my villa.   Both of you love sea-cool.

Læl.   He thinks that's too far off.

Nig.   Too far from where ?
He needs not Rome just now, nor Rome needs him.

Læl.   He's loth to leave it.

Nig.   Is he ?

Boy.   A butterfly !
A butterfly, mother, oh !

Nig. [*aside*].   Some one's in Rome.
But who ? I'd like to balk her.   [*To the boy*] Butterfly ?
Butterfly's flown away to the nice green woods,
Or maybe to the beach to find pink shells.
Would'st *thou* be glad to go ?

Boy.   Yes, yes.   Oh, come !

Nig.   Nay ; father 'tis must take thee.   Ask him well.
Lælia, there's some air come in Rome that's hurtful :
I know not what.   Coax Stellio and go soon.
Why dost thou gaze ?

Læl.   I feared—I thought—[*To girl child*]   See, baby,
Toss ball, Dulce will catch.   Toss it again.
Now brother's turn.   [*To Niger*] Speak low.   Give me thy
    meaning.
Why must we go ?

Nig.   Thou art so quickly scared.

I said my meaning.

Læl.   For Heaven's sake, say it plain.
Is it because—Is there something—any one—
For Stellio not to love me—that's in Rome ?

Nig. I've heard of no such thing. But—Well, be brave
One never knows ; there are chances ; men have whims.
Faith, all I do know's country air's the freshest.

Læl. And I am longing for it—longing so !
And the little ones would love it. But 'twas best,
I thought, not to tease Stellio, he being loth.
Wilt thou persuade him ?

Nig.   What ! thou dost not fear him ?

Læl. Not fear : he's kind. But he might think me vexing
Wives should not be importunate, thou know'st ;
It tries the husband's love. Do ask him, thou.

Enter STELLIO.

Boy [*runs to Stellio*]. Oh, father, take me to the shells.

Stell.   Why's that ?
[*To Lælia*]. Shouldst thou so ply thy needle after headache ?

Læl. Thou'rt right : I'll put it by, dear. Here's a seat.

Boy. The shells ! Come to the shells !

Stell.   Well, show me them
[*leads the child to the fountain*].

Boy. No, not the stone girl's shells : the pretty ones,
That the butterfly has gone for. Oh, the dove !
It threw the water at me.

Stell.   So will I. [*Sits by the fountain and splashes.*
There !

Boy.   So will I [*splashes*].   There, father !

Stell.   How we fight !

Boy.   But I can run [*runs away*] Oh ! Dulce has her lyre !
Sing Sing-song, Dulce.   [*To Niger*] Take me on thy knee.

SONG.

Sing-song, sing-song, little river :
Sleeping-time.
Sing-song, sing-song, leaves a-quiver :
Sing-song, breezes, breathing " Slumber,"
Sing-song, crickets, crackling " Ever,"
Sing-song, voices—oh, the number !—
With a drowsy chime,
Drowsy, drowsy, through our dozing ;
But the birds their eyes are closing,
Not a chirp till waking-time.

Læl.   The boy's asleep.

Boy.   No, most of me's awake [*sleeps*].

Læl.   He's tired.   And bed-time's come for sweetling here.
Come, nurses ; they're both ready.   I'll take baby.

Boy [*pushes his nurse away*].   Nurse go.   [*To Niger*] I'll let
thee carry me.

Nig.   And I will.

[*Exeunt Lælia, Niger, children, and nurses.*

Enter ÆONIA.

Æon.   Stellio.

Stell.   Thou ! Oh, shape of all my thoughts !

I am rash again : but never a soul can hear us.

But I'll be wary : thou shalt praise me. (*calls*) Girls !

Where is your mistress ?

  A slave.   With the children, Master.

I'll quick go call her.

  Æon.   Stop her : say " Not yet."

  Stell.   No, girl, hurry her not.   That's well, Æonia :

Sure, we may naturally change some words.

  Æon.   Stellio, I'm sick at heart.   I cannot bear it.

  Stell.   My darling, what ?

  Æon.   Never to be with thee—

Never ; for if we meet 'tis like vague ghosts,

Shadows and mocks of our divided selves :

Not thou my love and I thy love, but triflers,

Glib casual utterers of courteous nought.

Oh ! and trembling all the while lest cunning ears

Make who knows what of the lightest catch of breath ;

Lest eyes of the greedy wolf afoot for garbage

See the bait of scandal in a look, a flush,

A quiver that . . . tells the truth.

  Stell.   We fear them not.

  Æon.   We do.   We must.   Heavens, were our secret told !

I, thy betrothed, cold consecrate to honour,

That never yet have changed a lover's kiss,

Nor felt thy heart throb, nor sat hand in thine,

What should I be to the jeerers ?   Answer not :

Thou canst not say but what would make me sorer.

And, were no tongues so base as lie that lie,

Yet, the secret told—Oh, what? We two apart !
Always apart ! Thou tethered to Lælia ! I— !
Oh, Stellio ! and I never loved but thee !

    Stell. And that which, ere I knew thee, I thought love,
Was as a venture of a child's toy skiff
To his man's venture of an argosy
Where all his fortune's laden.

    Æon.   Do I doubt thee ?
No ; nor fear that thou'llt doubt me. We are sure.
But we *must* breathe : I will not bear this longer.

    Stell. Indeed we might meet oftener : by thy rules
There is no lady I so rarely see.
Be not so chary, and I'll be more prudent.

    Æon. Aye, but I'm weary of the prudence ; weary !
And then to be *caught !* Oh, there's no seemlier word.
Caught! like a larcenous slave found pilfering !
Like a loose girl at love behind mother's back !
Didst mark Æmilia ? There's Fonteia too :
She helped. That's worse than scorn—I hate her for it.

    Stell. She'll not think much to have helped us to ten words.
'Twas a natural charity.

    Æon.   That's its keen sting.
And then to think that more and more and more,
If this drag on, we'll need such charity . . .
And fear such scorn. Oh, hasten it.

    Stell.   If I could !

    Æon. I did but say it like sighing. We must wait.
And now I've come in thought to win us respite—

Some loosening of our thrall.   My Baian villa—
Thou hast heard I bought it—Baiæ would please Lælia ;
And nought so fit to float away her languors
As the soft breezes with the waves' breath in them.
Bring her and the children.   I'm your hostess, there :
It cannot be but, in the common life,
Thou and I many a time shall chance together,
Indifferent, unwatched.

    Stell.   Could this come true ?

    Æon.   Forth from her kin, none to umbosom her,
Save it were I, and none embittering,
Our winds may lightly drift her mind to our point.

    Stell.   Æonia !   Dare we?

    Æon.   What is there to dare?

    Stell.   *She* brought to *thy* house !

    Æon.   Where is this I stand ?
Is not this Lælia's home ?

    Stell.   Then, there's Æmilia.
She has some doubts ; this visit would enhance them.

    Æon.   No ; for 'twould show her Lælia does not doubt,
Who, bringing thee my guest, becomes our voucher.

    Stell.   The plan sounds fairly.   Best for Lælia's good,
No less than ours.   She'd, in a summer's dream,
Slip from the weary present of her tears
To a fair future to awake her in.
Yet—'Tis like treachery.

    Æon.   We're past that now.
Thy treachery was when first thy wayward thought,

Not then past check, was 'ware of flight from Lælia,
And yet thou didst not check, didst not shun *me ;*
Mine when I first bade thee not back to Lælia.
What's treachery now?   There's none : none possible.
The end that must be must be wrought, since willed.

Stell.   Thou dost but reason me to my own desire.
Oh, to be with thy presence filling the air !
To hear thee, see thee, hour by hour, be nigh thee !

Æon.   Pay me with silence : thanks go jarringly.

Stell.   I'll pay thee by and by : that will be never.
Thou'llt by and by give me full leave to love,
And what are thanks to love?

Æon.   Oh, then !

Stell.   Betrothed !
My own Æonia !

Æon.   Lælia tarries ; call her.

Stell.   But we'll not ask her that to-night.

Æon.   And wherefore ?

Stell.   She was sitting with the babes ; so happy.

Æon.   Yes ?
So happy is she ?   What am I ?

Stell.   We hope.

Æon.   Ah, love !   Yet—[*calls*] Girls, tell Lælia I must go.
Hark, Stellio, what I'll tell thee.   If thou waver——

Stell. [*interrupts*].   No.

Æon.   If, as seems, thou waver, choose.   Choose her.
I'll, so thou never breathe me prayer again,
So thou keep our dead love a nameless thought,

Past any's guess, past even thine own belief,
Not hate thee, not use memories, seem thy friend.
Choose her, I say : choose safety and good help,
Her, Caius, and the Lælii.   So farewell.

    Stell.   Thou hast not said all.

    Æon.   If not—[*pauses*]

    Stell.   Say to the end.

    Æon.   If thou do *not* choose her, if we keep troth,
Then I claim justice from thee—and my due place.
To which of us dost thou most need amends ?
Which of us bartered most against thy love ?
She could have wed past *thy* height ?   I as she :
And I forego the more who had more to gain.
She, an unmeaning girl who needed mate,
To wed thee coaxed her kin, shed baby tears ;
I, with ripe strength and treasured passionate heart,
To wed thee I have trampled on myself,
Stoopèd me to fears, to feigning, to shamed blushes,
Timorous to every eye lest it should read me.
Can thy debt to me be second?   No ; nor first :
'Tis all.

    Stell.   Thou hast my soul.

    Æon.   Else I would hate thee.
But set no Lælia where the right is mine :
Talk not " 'Twere our best speed ; but then there's Lælia,"
And " 'Twere thy due; but Lælia's due comes thwart : "
Again I tell thee, choose.   If for Æonia,
Balance no other's destiny with mine :

Reck of Æonia only—thee and me.

I go : thou'llt say to Lælia I was hurried.

Give her my bidding. Or give *not* [*going*].

 Stell.   Nay, tarry.

 Æon. This one hint more : if thou *do* give my bidding,

If she accept, her word should reach me soon.

Æmilia could not bid her slight me so,

As causelessly retract assent due given me.   [*Exit.*

     Re-enter Lælia.

 Læl. [*to the handmaids*]. Put work away. Good girls ; that's
   fitly wrought,

And daintily [*advances*]. What ! Has Æonia gone ?

 Stell. She spoke of haste.

 Læl.   But why, then, come at all ?

 Stell. To know if thy headache passed.

 Læl.   So kind ? That's pleasant.

I'd like to love Æonia.

 Stell.   There's a message.

 Læl. Yes ?

 Stell.   But thou'rt free to answer to thy mind.

I'll no way rule thee in it.

 Læl.   Nay, my love,

My will has not yet been apart from thine :

'Tis my dear joy it ever springs from thine—

Like the next bud on the first rose's stem.

Talk of no separate freedom ; that's its life.

 Stell [*aside*]. Poor child ! I cannot do it. [*To Lælia*]. Well
   then, no,

We'll tell her, no.

Lœl.   Is it Æonia asks,

And what, that thou'lt say no to ?

Stell.   Why, 'tis nought :

She goes anon to her new Baian villa,

And she'll have guests, and, neighbour-like, bid us.

Lœl. Baiæ ! Baiæ ! Sweet Numerius, think.

Must we indeed say no ? Prithee, love, yes.

Indeed Rome's air's too hot ; the babes grow pale.

Baiae's not lonely like our hills ; not far ;

So beautiful.   It need not be for long.

I see thou'rt wavering : let it be yes.

Stell.   When I said other 'twas in care for thee :

Lest it should irk thee.   But .... Let it be yes.

Lœl.   Dear heart, to grant my boon !   Yet—Let us counsel :

'Twould irk me, thou didst think ; will it irk thee?

Irk thee too much, I mean.   Dear, surely no?

We'll be so happy at bright happy Baiæ.

Not if it irk thee, though.

Stell.   'Tis my best hope.

Thine, maybe, too.

Lœl.   Thine and my hope !   We'll go !

She meant the children too ?

Stell.   Surely, with thee.

Lœl.   Would she had stayed for answer !   Is she far ?

Stell.   She went but that same moment as thou cam'st.

Lœl.   Oh, we can overtake her.   Run, dear love.

Stay her for me.

Stell.   To Baiæ; to Æonia.
'Tis by thy will then.   And indeed 'tis best.
Believe I seek thy happiness.

    Læl.   Say "Ours."

    Stell.   Yes, ours: I take thy omen: ours. [*Calls*] Æonia ! [*Exit.*

    Læl.   Forth from Rome's lurking ill that Niger said !
Forth, forth, to be new lovers at sweet Baiæ !

                            [*Exit following Stellio.*

END OF FIRST ACT.

ACT II.

Scene I. *A Terrace in Æonia's gardens at Baiæ.*

Enter Caius Cæsar, *from behind.*

Voice without. My Lord, how shall I folllow?

Cai.   Vault the fence.

Voice without. 'Tis high.

Cai.   Oh, wingless worm ! Tush ! Try again.
Again. Poor clod ! Invoke my name, and vault.

  Voice without. In the name of Caius Cæsar !

Cai.   So. Well sped ?
He has done it by my name. 'Tis a strange power....
Imperial Divinity : is it new?
Octavius had it : needs must he have had it,
Or not become Augustus, soul of Rome :

Enter Memnon.

And, since Divinity dies not, nor Rome's soul,
Tiberius was divine. And yet, I think,
The perfect emanation had not come
Till I.

  Memn. [*aside*]. Apollo keep his wits in poise !
This majesty's a dizzying thing.

Cai.   Alone ;

Men mine, and I some greater kind than men ;

Yet it was I that late lay worn with fever,

The weakest will-less thing that held a life.

What, who, am I ? 'Tis strange.   'Tis strange—Ah, Memnon !

I had forgotten thee.   There is thy post ;

Within that laurel clump.   Sharp ears, sharp eyes :

Then tell me all.

    Memn.   Finding thee here, Lord Caius?

    Cai.   They thou must spy on will be here ; not I.

Come home to me when there's news.   Or, if, perchance,

Thou hast learnt there's none to learn, come with that news.

    Memn.   I will.   But—If—I shall [*going.*]

    Cai.   Stay.   We have time.

What was't thou wouldst have said ?

    Memn.   'Twas but in zeal—

A fear lest, ignorant, I'd miss the signs.

But will and wariness shall teach enough,

Since Cæsar bids.

    Cai. [*aside*].   His eyes and ears are mine :

To see unwarned is often not to see,

To hear untaught the meaning's to hear false.

Why keep my eyes and ears too dull ?   I'll tell him.

[*To Memnon.*] Thou'rt faithful, Memnon ; and I love thee well ;

And, though tis not for me to unveil my path,

Nor fore-reveal my purpose, nor expound,

Yet will I show thee this.   I—thou hast known it—

Whether possessed, as poets and as seers,

And some say kings, into whom Apollo breathes,

Or of self-inspiration, see men's thoughts :

I have read secrets since I came to Baiæ.

    Memn.   So soon ! 'Twas yesterday.

    Cai.   What matters time ?

I do not search ; I see.   But, peace, and hear.

Stellio, that has for his of all sweet women

The sweet white wood anemone pure of the sun,

Turns him to that Æonia—is she called ?—

And Lælia's struck with the blight of their twin treason.

    Memn.   Is it possible ?

    Cai,   What's that to daze thee, fool,

That an honest wife, despised, should pine ?

    Memn.   Not that :

But 'tis a marvel if Æonia's tamed.

My lord, she's held unparagoned for coldness,

Pride's body and soul, exemplar for Diana :

And can she love ?

    Cai.   She can have languorous eyes,

Being unaware ; then, cautious suddenly,

Compel them into blankness, two mere crystals ;

Can, postured like stone Peace, perceptionless,

Thrill at a word he drops, note if he stirs :

Can stint to speak with him, and, speaking with him,

Be idly courteous, or be curt, or cold ;

Thus can she ; but not portion him common smiles,

Not show frank favour, talk with him like the rest ;

No, nor yet in his presence be at ease.

Memnon, she cannot : she's too much a lover.

Memn.   Last night while thou wast supping at Æonia's
I'd gossip chat with Dulce, Lælia's maid ;
Dulce knows nought, my lord.

Cai.   But Lælia knows.
My Lælia's changed to fitful, timorous, shy ;
She watched, and would not watch, and yet she watched.
Wretches !   They shall not break her heart.

Memn.   Hist !   Steps.

Cai.   No.   Where I stand I should see every comer.
Oh, that's this place's natural safeguard, man—
Bait of my trap to-day.   Up to this terrace,
(Come here and see,) there wind but those two paths—
One from the sea-cliff terrace near below us,
One from beside the lake.   They meet, thou seest,
Three minutes hence—time to prepare one's mien.

Memn.   No company can be with us ere we know :
True ; but we're sentries by the wall, in view.

Cai.   There's a secret.   Keep that ilex always left,
The olive right—that's range enough to walk,
And here's a seat in the angle—near thy laurels—
Now : there's the path : we see and are not seen.
But, blessings on it !   'tis no lurking-place :
An open terrace whither comes who will.
Why, 'tis the favourite summer-hall, no less ;
Most innocent, most public.   Long ago—
Long for I was a boy with the other boys,
Among them, like them.

Memn. [*aside*].   Now his thoughts are flown.

Cai. I was telling thee I had playmates in this villa.
This terrace was our trusty mischief-place ;
Here we shared orchard loot, devised our scrapes—
But always searched these laurels since, one day,
(Oh treachery !) their tutor hid and heard.
Thou, hide and hear.

Memn.   And if they come not hither ?

Cai. Tut ! all the house comes hither.   Spy on all.
Memnon, I'd crush a hundred lives to dust,
Ere one should stand in Lælia's sun a minute.

Memn. She is very dear to thee.   Would she were dearer.

Cai. How dearer?

Memn.   Wife, if it so seemed thee good.

Cai. That would spoil all.   'Tis a pleasant tenderness.
One comes, in the fire of noon, to, by a rill,
A favourite shelter where the pine scent's fresh,
A spot that's cool and still the thousandth time,
No memories in it but of cool sweet stillness :
My sense of her makes that in my throbbing life.
I am calmer, Memnon, surer of myself,
Because this kindness from the untroubled times,
This link of me to me, can hold within me.
Alter it, lose it ? no.

Memn.   'Twere pity ; true.

Cai. [*bursts into laughter*]. The merry end''twould make !
    Snatch her from Stellio !
He'd miss her, lost.   Aye, and fortune lost with her.

4

He'd writhe ; he'd writhe.   Then have him wed Æonia.
He'll hate her for his loss till she hate back.
Not banish them, though ; let them see Lælia throne it.

   Memn.   'Twere a good issue.

   Cai.   An impossible.

Jove so killed Semele.   I will not do it.
A stronger mate for me, more daring, loftier.
Æonia's fitter.

   Memn.   But, my lord, my lord !

   Cai.   My man, my man !   Say on.

   Memn.   Nay, there's no need:

Since now I see 'twas jest.

   Cai.   What's jest?   What's earnest?

Man's name and the gods' name, they, for all things done ;
And the gods' name is jest.   I'll take Æonia.

   Memn.   But that means wed her : she'll no less.

   Cai.   I know.

   Memn.   She's not of rank ; not meet as match for Cæsar.

   Cai.   Folly !   What woman is?   A rare prank that !—
Please Lælia, punish Stellio—Oh, 'twould punish !
I'll have him, times and times, at feasts and sports,
To look on his Æonia mine, all mine,
And he a thing she'll smile on, queen to serf ;
And her smiles will pierce his heart and blight and rasp !—
Like our hill winds that in the winter whiles
Bring us blue air and mellowness of the sun,
And stab us through the softness.   Oh good ! good ! [*laughs.*]

   Memn.   What gain to thee, oh Caius ?

Cai.   Ask me that !

Do I not rule as Jove and regnant gods?
Do they not punish? oftenest covertiy,
Often with published vengeance? 'Tis, in them,
Their nature and their pleasure : so in me.
Could the word duty stretch to them and me,
I'd say 'tis duty ; but, however named,
It hangs on sovereignty, is sovereigns' conscience.

Memn.   But, if the two plot love, there are two plot.
Vengeance on Stellio : but thou'lt wed Æonia.

Cai.   That might prove vengeance, too. Eh, Memnon? Eh

Mem.   If any made that flout but thou, I'd——

Cai. [*interrupts*].   chuckle.

Thou couldst no better, friend.   Well, keep close watch.
If thou learn aught within this hour or two,
Find me in the upper garden-house hard by.
That fence—thou'lt never vault it from this side.

Memn.   How must I do?

Cai.   Another secret, this :

Pass on behind the laurels where thou'lt lurk,
Thou'lt come where brambles half have hid the wall,
There stoop and grope ; there's a low aperture :
We made it for escapes.

Memn.   Amid the brambles?

Cai.   We trimmed them to our need.   That's long ago :
They'll be spread now ; they'll tear thee, make thee bleed.
Oh,good ! [*laughs*] And the nettles ! Oh, thou'lt pass, thou'lt pass :
But—but [*laughs*] I cannot speak. [*laughs*] Oh, could I see it!

Memn.   Does my lord hate me?

Cai.   Tush!   Thou know'st I prize thee.
'Tis but some smarts; thou'lt bear them for my sake.
And when is my hand closed to faithful—Ah!
Æonia coming to the trap!   She muses.
Too slim, too slim: but yet of the goddess sort.
Memnon!   A thought!   I'll give her thee for guerdon.

Memn.   To me!   A freedman!

Cai.   What I will, she must.
[*reflectingly*] But, wed her low, she's left in Stellio's reach.
Well, I'll take thought which way to will.   Be watchful.

                                    [*Exit Caius.*

Memn.   Aye, what it is this solitary power!
There be that envy it.   Too dizzying!   [*Exit into laurel thicket.*

                    Enter ÆONIA *musing.*

Æon.   Yet once I lived not needing love.   *I:* no.
Oh, 'twas but I as the worm that crawls and feeds
Is the winged rapture drunken with free air
That's playmate to the sunbeams.   Oh, this love!
Stellio, thou hast given me a soul.   [*sits*].

                                    Rose, fie!
Wilt thou touch lips I dare not let *him* touch?
Why, then, I'll pluck thee for our go-between.
Thus do I give him kisses—thus—thus—thus—
And thou shalt breathe them to him stealthily—Nay!
Thou shalt not.   Hence!   hence with thee to the earth!

                    [*Tears the rose.*]

Die in a hundred shreds, thou mockery.

Oh me ! Oh me ! When shall I be my Stellio's ?
When shall our loves leap meeting, fire to fire,
River to river, life blent into life ?
He is there ! Too slow, too slow.   Move, signal bough,

> [*Sets a bough moving.*

Set all thy leaves a-quiver, say I am here.

> [*Watches.*]

He has reached the bosk : I can go meet him now. [*Exit.*

Re-enter MEMNON *from the thicket.*

Memn.   They'll speak in sighs and murmurs ; I'm too far.
Aye, here's a nearer ambush as well hid.
There's time to peep, though, at their pretty welcomes.
How ! Could they spite so quickly ? Does she chide?
She walks apart and gathered in herself,
Like women brooding wrath ; he talks in heat,
Tosses clenched hands in a petulant despair.
What can have chanced in such a little minute ?
Aye, little minutes, they're the worst of rogues !
The big round hours plod, plod it, sober-foot,
The little minutes, ere they seem to have come,
Dart, and the venom's in the wound.   They're near.

> [*Exit into the thicket.*

Enter STELLIO *and* ÆONIA *in talk.*

Stell.   But say I yesterday was too unguarded,
This morn (the sorry actor !) rudely cold,
Could'st thou not now, for pity and sweet faith,

Have given me first love-comfort of three words ;
And not the blames till after ?

Æon. Aye, love-comfort !
A beggar can give alms ; he has his doles :
But ask from *me* love-comfort !

Stell. Is it so?
Do I nothing cheer thee, then, Æonia?
Oh, thou art cruel ! Never now we two,
Released into frank solitude, breathe freely,
But straight thou art angry.

Æon. When do we breathe freely ?
Oh, well for thee : thou hast an easy heart—
A balanced, too—Lælia, Æonia, Lælia—
Thou art piecemeal shares....and happy.

Stell. Am I happy?

Æon. Forgive me. I am petulant, unjust.
'Tis not my nature, bear me pityingly.
I am driven past reason with this racking stress,
This tyranny of our disunited lives.
To love so much and have so little of love,
To—There ! See there ! Not two poor minutes for us !
Never !

Stell. Who is it ?

Æon. 'Tis Fonteia. Is it ?

Stell. 'Tis Lælia : running.

Æon. Does she mean surprise ?
To take us unaware ?

Stell. She doubts us not.

Æon. She's tender of her ignorance, for, break it,
She'll be exposed thy canker, and, for cure,
Should ease thee of herself. She'll not.

Stell.   She will.
Thou hast not marked them, then. Metellus hopes.
She blushes and is grave.

Æon.   At dawn he went.

Stell. Heavens, no! But to return.

Æon.   His visit's ended.
Lælia besought him, called his love her hurt,
Said it had made thee almost doubt of her.
He told me. And I praised them. He has left her.

Stell. The fool! And she! Oh, thrice unhappy fool!
Herself undone as we are.

Æon.   Hush! she is here.

Enter LÆLIA.

Læl. News! guess ye who have come, that follow me?
Æmilia, Quintus, Marcus—in this grove!

Stell. And, prithee, what affair brings *them* to Baiæ?
Why sudden thus? 'Tis a most strange surprise.

Læl. Unwelcome, it would seem. I'm sorry for it.

Stell. Aye, find another woe: woes are thy food.
Who said unwelcome?

Æon.   I'll go welcome them.   [*Exit.*

Stell. [*paces up and down; then*] Lælia, what does their
     coming mean? Reply;
I claim the truth.

Læl.   I understand thee not.
I know no meaning.

Stell.   Thou hast summoned them.
Say wherefore.

Læl.   I have *not.* Why should I, husband ?
I will not think that, being by thy side,
I need to summon any.   If I thought it—
Why, still I would not think it.

Stell.   Oh, spare flouts.
Else shall I know that they have come thy spies ;
And loathe thy treachery.

Læl.   I to risk thy harm !
Nay, thou'lt not think it.   Trust me, husband, still :
And if thou take away thy love, yet trust me.
Indeed, indeed, not even to myself
Have I once blamed thee—Nay, and wherefore blame ?
Thou never hast done fault to me.   I love thee.

Stell.   Alas, my Lælia !   And I wring thy heart !

Læl.   Sometimes ; a little ; but I knew 'twas nought,
And now thou hast said it all the pain is gone.
But, dear, let's not talk now.   I might seem moved ;
Then, who knows what surmises?

Stell.   True ; not now.
This is no time—We must talk afterwards—
Perchance I meant not as thou—'Tis no matter.
This is no time for more : thou'rt very right.

Æon. [without].   Came you from Formiæ ?

Æmil. [without].   From Formiæ.

Æon. [*without*].   'Tis dusty travelling, surely.

Æmil. [*without*].   That, indeed.

Æon. [*without*].   But 'tis not very long.

Æmil. [*without*].   Not many hours.

Re-enter ÆONIA, *with* ÆMILIA, QUINTUS, *and* MARCUS.

Stell.   I greet thee, honoured mother : brothers, greeting.

Æmil.   My son, I greet thee well !

Quint.   Good-day.

Marc.   Good-day.

Stell.   You're sudden like the quickening showers of spring,
Welcome and warningless.

Æmil.   We ne'er planned coming,
But came, being bid.

Æon.   Pray you all sit to rest.   [*All sit.*

Marc.   Thanks : 'tis a goodly rest-place.

Quint.   Cool and sheltered.

Æon.   Yes ; the high air comes fresh, and, all day long,
Somewhere there's shadow.   We spend much time here.

Æmil.   Who do ?

Æon.   My guests : and gladly I with them.

Stell.   You gaze upon the prospect.   Is't not fine ?

Marc.   'Tis very pleasant : true.

Quint.   Most bountiful.

Æon.   What news bring you from Rome ?

Marc.   There's none we know.

Stell.   News is for wakeful ears : Baiæ's a dream.

Æon.   What's Formiæ ?   A dream ?

Stell.   Marcus is guessing.
IIe thinks he's asked a riddle.
Marc.   No, indeed.
But Quintus might mean answering, or our mother;
I did not know Æonia singled me.
I pray her pardon.
Æon.   That's an easy boon :
So little wrong being done me.
Marc.   Thanks.
Stell.   For prospects—
Look, sheer above the water, that high shelf,
Cut in the cliff—you passed it mounting hither—
'Tis from that terrace there's the gem of prospects.
Æon.   Aye, there one has the unlimited expanse.
Stell.   One has the long smooth curves of all the shore,
The hills, the heaven of the blue bay outspread,
The irradiate isle that half seems made of sky—
Oh, 'tis like sorceries !   You must see the terrace.
'Tis Lælia's favourite haunt.
Æmil.   Alone ?
Stell.   That pine—
The single one—shades an old ruined tomb,
Whereof there's a strange tale.
Æmil.   Why, son-in-law,
Thou fondlest this domain as 'twere half thine.
Stell.   The wife and babes, how fare they, Quintus ? Well ?
Quint.   Well ; very well.
Stell.   At Formiæ, are they ?

Quint.   Yes.

Læl.   Mother, who was't thou said'st that bade thee come ?

Æmil.   Thou'rt sure 'twas not thy hostess nor thy husband ;
Then who but Caius, child ?   " Things needed us "—
That's what his streaming post brought for our waking.
Now he explains like two-edged oracles,
This way and that, and nought.

Læl.   One of his freaks.

Æmil.   Most   freaks   begin   from   somewhere,   somewhere
     tend.

Stell.   True, the jest's not but strange.

Quint.   We think it strange.

Æon.   Is it so strange to wish good company ?
Let me be strange then, for I too wish yours.
Give me to-day, and all the days you can.

Æmil.   We thank, but cannot use, thy courtesy.
We are guests to Caius.   Lælia, seek me soon.

Læl.   This afternoon, dear mother.

Æmil.   We'll take leave.

Æon.   So soon ?   At least not here, revered Æmilia ;
My duty is to attend thee to my gates.   [*Exeunt omnes.*

                 Re-enter MEMNON.

Memn.   Æmilia dropped a paper. [*searches*]   I am sure—
Yet—Ah ! 'tis here ! [*reads*]   " Things need thee, need thy sons.
Come."   Nought : no prize to take to Caius, this,
His last night's missive ; merely owls to Athens.
Well, I have heard enough to fill his ears.

                              [*Exit through the thicket.*

ACT II.

SCENE II. *The same: later in the day.*

Enter from the thicket CAIUS CÆSAR *and* MEMNON.

Cai.   Didst thou hear voices?

Memn.   No, not yet, Lord Caius.

Cai.   Yet !   Why, they're past.   They seemed to sigh in the
air.

Some one's to perish.   Stellio?   No.   Æonia?
I know not.   What didst *thou* hear?

Memn.   Not a breath.

Cai.   Of course.   Thou hast the poor five mortal senses,
How shouldst thou go beyond them?

Memn.   Verily not.
I use my five poor senses mortal ways,
And can no more ; and I'd not dare to try.

Cai.   That's wisdom, Memnon, past philosophers,
Who aim to measure in their little brains
The purposes of Heaven that made them fools.
Art sure thou saidst thy message plain?

Memn.   Most sure.

Cai.   Yet no one's here.   What didst thou tell the girl?

Memn.   That she must privily give her mistress word,
And her mistress come here privily—I see her.

Cai. Lean forth. Are the others on the terrace still ?

Memn. They're all just so as we, five minutes since,
Still saw them from thy garden-house above—
All save but Lœlia ; and there's in her place
Dulce that minds the children.

Cai.   What does Stellio ?

Memn. Still helps Fonteia pelt the babes with flowers.

Cai. Æonia ?

Memn.   With those visitors still. Those came,
So Dulce says, by boat, and wait their rowers.

Cai. No matter what they wait, so they but wait
And keep hence those I need not. Stand away ;
They'll see thee if thou lean so far.

Enter LÆLIA.

Lœl.   Hail, Cæsar !

Cai. Dear child, I greet thee well. Thou'rt pale.

Lœl.   Oh, no ;
Why hast thou sent for me so strangely, Caius ?

Cai. I felt a mind to talk with thee ; that's all.
Go, dear, and choose a seat by the myrtles there ;
I'll follow thee. [*Lœlia goes.*] [*To Memnon*] Keep screened and
     in the range ;
If any mount the path, toss arms in the air.

Lœl. [*aside*]. What can it be? Kindness, I know ; he's kind;
But—Oh, he cannot help me and harm Stellio.

Cai. [*sits by Lœlia*]. Sweetling, my sister by my love to thee,

Now speak as to thy brother, king, and god :
Show me thy heart.

Læl.   What wouldst thou know, dear Caius ?

Cai.   Art thou content with Stellio ?

Læl.   That's no word :
I love him.

Cai.   But he's false.

Læl.   He is not.   No !

Cai.   Not with Æonia ?   Ah !   Thou canst not speak.

Læl.   He—She's so beautiful—No man but gazes—
And he, maybe—I do not think 'tis love.

Cai.   Why has she brought ye here ?

Læl.   No ill in that.

Cai.   He was a beast to come.

Læl.   How darest thou say it ?
He came for my sake, at my urgency.

Cai.   Oh, Lælia ! oh !

Læl.   He loathed to come from Rome.

Cai.   They are lovers sworn.

Læl.   Oh, no !   I tell thee no.

Cai.   Say thou hast never thought it.   Swear so much.

Læl.   I'm not so wise as never to be jealous :
But I trust him, Caius.

Cai.   So ?   That do not I.

Læl.   Oh, know him better : listen to a secret :
He did so little come for what thou sayst
That then in Rome there was some evil woman
Who—might perchance have lured him.   Her he left :

Not willingly, but his heart was brave for me.
Must I not thank him? For my sake he left her :
Mine, not Æonia's.

    Cai.　　　　　He has duped thee, child ;
Dressed thee a scarecrow of a bodiless love
To frighten thee to his Æonia's arms.

    Læl. He did not ; he not even guessed I knew ;
'Twas Niger told me.

    Cai.　　　　　*He* in the stratagem !

    Læl. Thou art too suspicious ; basely.

    Cai.　　　　　　　　Am I, dear ?
I would I were.

    Læl.　　　To-day, this very day,
He, as awaking in a love remorse,
Cried to me from his heart. I am content.

    Cai. [*goes from her*]. That some such pure soul loved me !
    Oh, thrice more,
Would God 'twere in me to love one like her !
My simple darling ! Wretches ! What's to do ?
She's fenceless, guileless. Leave her to them thus ?
Spare her the surgeon's pangs I'd give to-day,
And have her perish to-morrow ? [*Goes back to Lælia*] Tell me,
    sweet—
Oh, tell me first the secret of those tears.
Content, and weeping ? Canst not trust me, Lælia ?
My darling, I am changed to most : alas !
Caius the boy is gone that had a heart,
As hearts are in mankind ; only, sometimes,

Caius the Emperor remembers him.
Thou dost remember him ?

Lœl.   Tenderly, Caius.
And so that I believe he's not gone far :
Caius the Emperor can fetch him back,
Old self to new : and will.   But the new's good too.

Cai.   Dear, old or new self, thou of all the world,
If none else could, couldst trust my guardian care.
Tell me this much : grant that those two were traitors,
What destiny for them were most thy good ?

Lœl.   Their destiny ?

Cai.   If thou would'st have them die ;
If live in shame ; if—I could tell thee ways,
But thou'rt too pale.

Lœl.   Promise me, none of the ways.

Cai.   'Tis only if they're traitors to thee.

Lœl.   Promise.
Caius, for my sake.   Oh, for justice's sake !

Cai.   Cease this alarm.   By my own sacred name,
They shall be safe, I'll lift no finger at them :
Till thou aver them traitors : never till then.

Lœl.   That's a good promise.   And take no more thought.
I'm happy enough, and look to be more happy.

Cai. [*aside*].   Best take her from him ere he break her heart.
[*To Lœlia*].   Lælia, be consort to me, if thou wilt.
Fear me not ; I'll be very gently kind :
Thou'lt soothe my moods, and cheer me girlishly,
And use thy pretty influence that's my balm.

Let the two pair, and hide out of our sight
In squalid exile, where they'll curse each other ;
Thou, be the worshipped woman of all earth.
Lælia, 'tis that we'll do.

Læl.   I am Stellio's wife.

Cæsar, have I thy leave to go ?

Cai.   No.   Wherefore ?

Has the thought frighted thee ?

Læl.   Anger me no more.

[*Bursts into tears*].   Oh, Caius ! and thou badst me love thee
    so !

Cai.   Patience, dear heart.   Come, I'll not vex thee longer :
We'll end our talk.   Go to thy mother, dear ;
She waits thee in my house.   We'll talk to-morrow.

Læl.   Not as to-day, then.

Cai.   'Twill not be to-day.

Læl.   Not of—not of thy consort.   Hear me, Caius,
I'll loathe thee if thou speak of that again.

Cai.   Good girl.   Thou hast answered valiantly.   Now go.

Læl.   Farewell : I'll to my mother.   [*Exit Lælia.*

Cai.   Memnon !   Hist !

Must I go to him ? [*Goes to Memnon*] Art thou deaf, man ?

Memn.   Pardon.

I did not hear thee call.

Cai.   Didst muse of the pricks ?

Now which last more, the nettle-blobs or the thorn-pricks ?

Memn.   I can feel neither, both being in thy service.

Cai.   Thy skin must tingle.   Well, well, that's all done.

5

Henceforth thou'lt pass our tunnel, to and fro,
Like a sparrow through wide air.   Much like, indeed ;
For sparrows spy and tell, they say.   Come, Memnon,
To my garden-house.

    Memn.   What to spy there, my lord ?

    Cai.   To keep an eye upon the sea-cliff terrace,
When they stir there, heigh ! to the laurels here !
The trap will fill.   Lælia's gone seek her mother :
The pair will snatch such chance for conference ;
For, by thy tale, Æmilia has so borne her
As must have set them pondering of their case.

                              [Exeunt into the thicket.

ACT II.

SCENE III. *The same.*

Enter ÆONIA and FONTEIA in talk.

Font. And that's the history. She vowed she knew it.

Æon. 'Tis a graceless tale.

Font.   The likelier to be true.

Æon. That jest's too harsh. And gossip's mostly false.

Font. And so are echoes; yet first some voice rings right.
But come, Æonia, we are here alone:
Wilt thou ne'er tell me?

Æon.   What dost ask?

Font.   Thou know'st.

Æon. Love tales again? I have none.

Font.   I would 'twere fact
Unless thou'dst pitch thy love to better profit.

Æon. Prithee leave talk of me. Didst note, just now,
How red Laurentia turned at Otho's name?

Font. Oh, but they say she aims at Caius.

Æon.   She !
Brave aspiration ! To be Rome's first matron,
Consort of him that rules the very world:
All greatest, noblest, strongest, heaped below him,

Jostling for room where the sunshine of him falls,
And he to make their fates by any word :
And then he sets her by him—that one woman.
And mere Laurentia hugs a hope of that !

Font.   She has powerful kindred, lineage, wealth.

Æon.   I know.

Be sure she has made *my* lowliness feel *that.*
Yet she's low too to some as fair as she.
Rome has of such a marriageable dozen,
All nobler, wealthier, with more potent kin,
Most of them very like her ; where's her chance ?

Font.   Why was thy birth not sorted to thy beauty ?
The she-Cæsar *thou* wouldst make !

Æon.   Better, far better,
Than thousands adulating Cæsar's wife,
One's love at home.

Font.   And what's *One's* other name ?

Æon.   Tush ! babbler ; I but spoke of possible things
As thou didst of impossible : mine, as thine,
A swift hypothesis of talk.

Enter STELLIO.

Font.   Æonia,
I fear for thee lest thou and——Here comes Stellio.

Stell.   Both tempted here so soon this afternoon !
Then 'tis my favouring genius prompted me.

Font. [*aside*]. Mine should have prompted me to stay away.
[*Aloud.*] Sit, then, and help us gossip.

Stell.   Let me listen. [*Sits by Fonteia.*

Stell. [*after a pause*]. This golden stillness keeps us all a-
dream.

Font. Not me. Æonia dreams.

Æon.   I would I did.
What's worth the being awake?

Font.   Art thou transformed?
Thou to turn petulant ! That's not thy part :
Thou'rt all unlike Life's tetchy mutineers,
That make a lip but mean no harm, good souls.

Stell. But does Fonteia think no sadness true?

Font. None where no sorrow is.

Æon.   Oh, cease dispute !
Somewhere we need some peace.

Font.   Why, here's no war.
Save that song-duel : listen. But 'tis strange
That we so love birds' merely iterant notes
And think in them monotony never stale.

Æon. But these are shrill. Why must they make us hear
them ?
They pierce our ears.

Font.   I'll fly then, ere I'm deaf.
No, follow me not : I'd liefer be alone.

   [*Sings, going*]. Where young men and women be
                      Talk should have one more than two ;
                      One and one, the other—who ? [*Exit.*

      [*without*] Who but Love to make the three.

Æon. [*clasps her hands passionately*]. Oh ! oh ! Gods kill us !

Stell.   Dear, take heart, take heart.
There's yet no certain peril.

Æon.   There's far worse.
Oh, I could front an open desperate peril,
Could dull my enemies' enjoyed revenge,
Making it poor by smiling : pangs I'd bear,
Death, shame....for thee, my Stellio. But thus, thus!
Canst *thou* endure to the end? *Canst* thou?

   Stell.   I love.

   Æon. [*gives him her hand*].

   Stell. Still brooding, dearest?

   Æon.   Only quiet for joy.
Thou hast comforted me, Stellio.

   Stell.   'Twas not hard.
I spoke my thought that sums up all my thoughts,
And told thee what thou couldst not have in doubt,
And lo! thine effluent smile. Then, sweet, good courage :
We cannot be ill-fated, loving so.

   Æon. [*rises and walks about restlessly*]. But the weariness!
    Apart still ; always apart !
And feign, and feign, and rot our hearts with feigning !
And now suspected, pried on, dogged, in risk.
Taunted—thou heardst Æmilia.

   Stell.   But too well.
And yet she said not much. We must take counsel.

   Æon. And light Fonteia !

   Stell.   Nay, she shoots at random :
What matter for Fonteia? Say, dost think—

Or art thou overwrought for counsel now?

Æon. We'll talk : 'twill not be soon again we can :
We must be still more strangers, never alone :
They'll set their Lælia on to dog us more.

    Stell. She does it meaningless.

    Æon.   Perchance.   No, scarcely.
But now there are bloodhounds on the scent.

    Stell.   We are warned.

    Æon. Yes, and our safety is——

    Stell.   Wilt thou not end?

    Æon. Only farewell.

    Stell.   Æonia !

    Æon.   We'll not say it.
We could not say it.   But farewell *is.*

    Stell.   No.
Better risk all and perish.

    Æon.   Not together :
They'd not let *that* be.

    Stell.   Why, but all's not lost.
For our betrothal 'tis most sure they guess not,
And what surmise of love they have we'll blunt.
I'll fool it with Fonteia ; thou, go careless.
I must be Lælia's more too.

    Æon.   For how long?
See, is farewell not here?   I desolate,
Mocking indifference : thou blank nought for me,
Lælia's, Fonteia's, any one's but mine.
Love in our hearts ; yes, but kept bond and numb ;

A load to bury with us ; never aught more.

   Stell.   If I thought that I'd live no hour past now.

   Æon.   And why not end the struggle so, we both?

Look, the wide quiet sea ; room there, and rest :

So near, so easy—just a minute down—

A minute hand in hand, let who will see—

To the terrace ledge—a leap—and we'd kiss first :

We should be forth from all this coil and fever ;

Forth, and none with us in the stillness. Well?

   Stell.   Never to have fulfilment of our love !

Not even one day ours! Not yet. Not yet.

We cannot die.

   Æon.   We cannot die.

                   [Voices below sing.]

     The sun's the heart of the sky o'erhead.

       Only one sun though the sky's so great.

     If the sun never came the sky would go dead.

       But the moon may shine when the sun dawns late.

     And, oh, my love and my loving one,

     Thou art my heart and my single sun :

       And, oh, my sun in my passion's great sky,

       The moon and the stars can do nothing but die.

   Æon.   There's singing.

The fisher-folk are merry on their beach.

   Stell.   Merry? I thought not so. I scarcely heard them.

   Æon.   Nor I.

   Stell.   Hast thou planned aught?

Æon.   Ah, no ; ah, no.
We're past device.   Lælia will never free thee.

Stell.   Sometimes I've feared she'll fret ; and die away.

Æon.   No, no : these toys of creatures outwear stronger.
Their hearts have no big throbs that kill.   But *fear ?*
Say *hope :* save that the hope's not possible.

Stell.   '*Twas* fear : to-day 'twere hope.

                    [*A voice below sings.*]
          The net was torn, the fisher was woe,
              And it held but only a shell,
          And " Why was I born to be spited so ? "
              But soon it was well, it was well.
          The net was torn for a round rich pearl,
          Didst thou vex and spite me a while, fair girl ?
              Gain of a pearl was harm to the net,   ˙
              Fair girl, my ring's on thy finger yet.

Stell.   Dear, wilt thou hear me ?

Æon.   What doubt of that ?   Why ask ?

Stell.   I have a thought....
Well-nigh past speaking.

Æon.   Hush !   'Tis in thy voice.
Is it of Lælia ?   Speak it not.   But how ?

Stell.   We'd be close actors, fall, as unaware,
In every ambush, answer every lure,
So using each that spyers, self-convinced,
Should be pleased converts of our harmlessness ;

In Rome 'tis thou and Lælia should be cronies,
I the mere husband third ; so we'd for long,
Inure their confidence.

>   *Æon.*   So much we'll do.

>   *Stell.* So much and we were safe.   Then....if she died

....Some slow and gentle death....We could not.   No.

>   *Æon.* Let's think. Hush ! Let me think. Hast thou
>   planned it long?

>   *Stell.*   Never till now.

>   *Æon.*   We have not time to think.

No !   Oh, my Stellio, how to thank thee for it !
Now, come what may, I know that in thy world
There's only I alone.   But put it by :
We will not.   No ; not poison.   Let her live :
She has not thee.   Mine in thy very soul !

>   *Lælia's voice* [*without in the thicket*].   What, Memnon !
>   Wherefore here ?

>   *Memnon's voice* [*without in the thicket*].   By chance—yes
>   chance,

I come to—I must make haste now to Cæsar.

>   *Stell.* [*not having heard the voices*].   What shall we do ?

> *Enter* LÆLIA *from the thicket.*

Æon. [*not having heard the voices*].   Shall we have choice to do?
We are waves the winds will drive.

>   *Læl.* [*aside*].   How grave they are !
> They do not see me yet.

>   *Stell.*   " Things needed them."

What was in Cæsar's mind?

Æon.   Perchance not we.

Who could arraign us to him?   How should—Lælia !

Stell.   Here! Whence?   How daredst thou?

Læl.   Is to startle thee crime?

And, dear, I meant it not.

Stell.   Make me no glozings.

I know my enemy, smooth serpent, now :

Sting openly at last.

Læl.   What have I done?

Æon.   Oh, end hypocrisies and take thy triumph,

Or hadst thou comrades in thy hiding-place

That wait to hear the prettiness of thy feints?

Læl.   What meanest thou, Æonia?   Hiding-place?

Why should I hide, or why have comrades hidden?

I come from Cæsar's house.   Mother, strolled out,

Left word I'd find her in his sea-brink porch,

And on my way I, lured by these briar roses,

Pushed through a wrecked and long abandoned land,

And saw, through new-pruned thorns, an earthy mouth

Yawn in the bank : whither the grotto led,

When I explored, was to this bosk, was here.

And I, Æonia, thought not of detections :

Nor could, unless by thy too strange reproach.

Æon.   Hark, Lælia : how thou cam'st, or why, I care not ;

Spy all thou wilt thou'lt make us no more dreads.

Thou shalt have found the truth.   Aye, take it to thee ;

And know we reek not if thou achieve our deaths,

So we breathe some few moments—bold with love.

We love. Dost thou hear? We love. We are troth-plight
 lovers.

Læl. Oh, make her hush.

Æon.   For months we have been betrothed ;
For months we have schemed deliberate, toiled, and tricked,
To wed thee out of the way by, thou shouldst think,
Thine own desires. Thou to dream Stellio jealous !   ·
I tell thee we two chose the artless youth,
Thy shy Metellus, we, ere he, untaught,
Guessed that his childish amity meant a wish.
Know it : we're tired : avenge thee.

Læl. [*to Stellio*].   Speak to me ! Speak !
Hast thou heard her ?

Stell.   'Tis thy right to be revenged ;
Thou hast the power ; we will not ask for mercy.
I am sorry, too, that thou and I part so,
Thou made my enemy : but I deserve it.
Prithee no vain reproach : go, leave us now.

Æon. Wilt thou not leave us? Not for so short respite
As while thou'lt tell thy wrongs? Why dost thou gaze?
Wilt thou know more? Thou would'st not have lived long.
This very now—dost note?—here, where thou hast found us,
We planned thy ailing death.

Stell.   Not that ; not planned.

Æon. Oh, let her have her fill of knowledge now !
[*To Lælia*] A slow and gentle death; that was the thought.
We were merciful : we pitied thee : we pitied.

Dost hear me?

Stell.   Judge her not by what she says.
If aught was dreamed—if that wild thought was slipped—
'Twas not Æonia's, Lælia; blame not her.
Denounce me for thy murderer, if thou wilt,
Not her.   I swear it, Lælia, she forbade me.

Lœl.   Husband! [*gasps*] I *should* die.   [*Exit Lælia.*

Stell. [*following*].   Lælia! Lælia!

Æon. [*catches Stellio's hand*].   Wait.

Stell.   She'll harm herself.

Æon.   Wait.

Stell.   But—Who know's what's her
    purpose!
Nay, let me follow in time.

Æon. [*still holding him back*].   Stand thou with me.
The gods are portioning our three destinies;
Life for us two together, or her revenge.
In her heart is the choice : and the gods guide her.
Wait the award, I say, and hinder not.

[*A pause.   Then confused shouts from the shore below, out of
                        sight.*

Æon.   Listen!   I think 'tis done.

Stell.   I hear mere noise.
The fisher folk are noisy when they laugh.

        [*The shouting from below increases.*

Stell.   Hush!   Listen!   Said they....

Æon.   Yes.

A voice shouting below, nearer than the others. What's chanced?

Another voice more distant. A woman's drowned.

Fonteia. [*calling without*]. Stellio! come! Stellio! Stellio!

Voices approaching confusedly. Stellio! Find Stellio.

Stell. [*shouts over the terrace wall*]. What! What news! Who needs me?

[*To Æonia*]. I must perforce go hear.

Æon.   We both should go.

Voices below confusedly. Look! Is it the body? No. Yes. Out to sea.

[*Exeunt Stellio and Æonia.*

ACT II.

SCENE IV. *The same.*

Enter STELLIO, ÆONIA, FONTEIA, NEDA, EUTHYMUS.

Stell. [*to Æonia*]. And yet we were not wise to turn back
  hither.
It but postpones the meeting.

Æon. [*to Stellio*].   And seems flight.
I know not why we did it.—Hush ! They'll hear.
Fonteia, we're all dazed with this strange news ;
Let's gather our wits, and then go use them well.

Font. We must. Yet what's to do but mourn ?

Æon.   There's nought.

Neda. Oh, come ! Look ! Look ! The divers sure have
  found her.
Alas, no !

Euth. No. And the boats are hauling off.
[*To Stellio*] Dear master, give the strangling tear-fit vent :
'Tis best.

Stell. I would I could ; but horror numbs me.

Font. Alas ! Alas ! Poor Lælia ! [*sobbing*].

Enter ÆMILIA, QUINTUS, MARCUS, *with attendants and
  slaves of the Lælii and a throng of fishers and peasants.*

Æmil.   Aye, they're here.
I knew they had fled us.   Seize the murderers.

Stell.   What's this?   What murderers, Æmilia?

Æmil.   Thou.
She.

Æon.   Marcus, has this sorrow hurt her brain?

Marc.   How did my sister find her death, Æonia?

Æon.   I pray thee, tell us.

Æmil.   Out ! pale hypocrite !
Hear, all of ye : they, these two murderers,
Hurled Lælia from the cliff.   [*Groans and clamour.*

Stell.   'Tis false.—A dream.
We were not there.

Quint.   Prove that.

A voice in the throng.   Tear them to rags !

Another voice.   The sweet young pretty lady !

Another.   Our young mistress !

Another.   Stone them !

Another.   She never spoke but for sweet words.

Another.   I dandled her a child.

Another.   Oh, their hard hearts !

Another.   And her dear innocent babes made motherless !

Several voices.   Seize them !   Destroy them !   What are we
   waiting for ?

Stell.   Silence.   Be still.   I bid ye hear me speak.
                              [*Crowd hushes.*
[*To Æmilia*]. Now, madam, let me ask for some sane answer.
Who says we were with Lælia then ?

Æmil.   You were.

Quint. 'Tis like.

Marc.   'Tis like.

Æmil.   Some of you there, you fishers,
You saw her fall ; saw you who hurled her down ?

A fisherman. Not I.

2nd fisherman.   Not I.

3rd fisherman.   Our backs were mostly turned.
We heard the splash and ran to it. She rose once.

4th fisherman. I've heard of some can swear they saw her
    hurled.

Stell. If there be—be there but one who says that lie,
Go fetch the witness.

Æmil.   Aye, fetch witnesses.
But seize them now. On to them, men ! [*The Lælii's servants
                                            advance.*

Stell.   Back, fellow ! [*strikes
  one who has laid his hand on Æonia.*

Quint. On to him, men !

Voices.   Aye, on to them ! [*they surround
  Stellio and Æonia.*]

Stell.   Euthymus !

Euth. Here ! With a staff, too, some of them shall feel.
Make way ! make way ! [*struggles with some of the Lælii's
    people who thrust him back.*]

A voice.   Hale them to where they did it.
They may leap after her.

Voices laughing and shouting. Aye, aye, that may they.

6

To the cliff!   Seize them, you there!

Æon.   Æmilia!   Lælii!

Will you have us murdered?

Marc.   Pinion them; hurt them not.

We'll punish them presently.

One of the Lælii's servants.   Sir, make them leap.

Voices.   Aye, aye; that's justice.

Stell. [*to a servant*].   Dare not touch her, villain.

Back!   Touch her not.

Quint.   Yield, ere they tear thee piecemeal.

Æon.   Resist no longer, Stellio.   We can die.

Neda. [*clings to Æmilia's knees*].   Oh, mercy!   mercy!   spare

my dear dear lady!

Enter CAIUS *and* MEMNON.

Cai.   Peace, brawlers, peace!   Leave screaming, girl!   Peace,

all!

Hands down, you there: fall back. [*Those who were pressing
round Stellio and Æonia fall back silently*].   Good mob,
make room. [*The crowd scatters*].

What's this irreverent tumult near my house?

Æmil.   One, Caius, of our making; that thou'lt praise.

These are our prisoners, that murdered Lælia.

Cai.   Murdered her!   Art thou crazy?   Who are these?

Are they not loyal Stellio, pure Æonia?

Æmil.   We do believe thou hast guessed their practices.

Cai.   Practices, practices!   These are virtuous souls;

What jealous slanderer says they wronged thy daughter?

I tell thee Lælia's self, few hours ago,

Here, talking with me in sole confidence,
Dispelled the idle doubts, showed Stellio true,
Showed proud Æonia's honourable pride,
And all she spake was sunshine like herself;
"She was happy enough and looked to be more happy."

 Æmil. Oh, my dear child !

 Cai.   Poor mother, be consoled :
Belike she has her hope; she is more happy.

 Marc. We think this couple played her false.

 Cai.   Fie ! Fie !
Still so suspicious.

 Quint. We have seen her grieving.

 Cai. In Rome ; not at her friend Æonia's here.
To-day she said the secret of that grief,
Telling it me for joy.   There was—at Rome—
An evil woman, beauteous, seeming pure,
Who (Lælia said it) might perchance have lured him :
Because of her did Stellio haste from Rome—
For Lælia's sake (she said it) at her prayer,
"Part loth," she said, "but his heart was brave for me."

 Æmil. Who was this woman ?

 Cai.   Ah ! The riddle's there.
But why'lt thou heed her, if she won him not ?
"Me, not Æonia," that was Lælia's boast ;
And well she knew, she said, Æonia's honour,
And how she was too proud for treachery.
Will you take Lælia's witness, mother, brothers ?

 Æmil. Why went I forth just now before she came

And now she can never tell me.   Her own voice,
Her own revealing eyes for mine to probe ....
Then I should know.

Marc.　　　　　　Since Caius is convinced,
Mother, belike we, too, should—

Æmil. [*interrupts him*].　　　　Told she all?
Had she learned all to tell?

Marc.　　　　　　The girl, my Cæsar,
So simply worshipped Stellio that, from him,
Denial of a thing she that while saw
Would seem more credible than that he lied.
And, note, 'tis shown when, by that unknown woman,
She suffered grief in Rome, she cloked it all;
Secret till owning it came like his praise.

Cai.　Ye are too suspicious; basely.

Quint.　　　　　　But say this,
Oh, Caius, thou who heardst her, seemed she clear?
Did she indeed convince thee?   I'll trust that.

Cai.　Have I not spoken?   Yes, I am convinced.

Marc.　By this 'twould seem we have wronged Æonia much.

Quint.　And Stellio was, more than most husbands, constant.

Æmil.　But Lælia's dead.

Cai.　　　　　　Thou knowest my garden-house:
I see that terrace from it.   Aye, or no?

Æmil.　I know thou canst.

Cai.　　　　　　I saw her then, I tell thee.
Just then from the garden-house I looked a-down—
'Twas chance—and she came there.   And then she fell.

None saw save I. She was alone.

Æmil.   But, fell?

Cai.   Through stretching for a crimson gillyflower.
I tell thee none was near her, none in sight.

Font.   Cæsar, if I dare speak.

Cai.   Speak.

Font.   I was with them.
I left them here few minutes ere it chanced:
Here found them then.   They could not have been nigh her.

Cai.   Woman! how dost thou dare thy testimony,
As if the Augustus ask corroborance?
Check thine unhallowed tongue.   Thou, Stellio, speak.

Stell.   Cæsar, what shall I speak, save but to thank thee.
Thyself hast judged.

Cai.   Æonia, speak.

Æon.   What words?
I have no need to speak, being innocent.
Only I too give thanks to Cæsar's justice.

,   *Cai.*   Will ye pardon this sad mother grief made wild,
These brothers who, by care for her you've lost,
Have blindly rushed against your innocences?
Pardon them, since *ye* loved their Lælia too,
You both, had others been like you accused,
Might not have missed like passion in her name.

Æmil.   I am sorry we in any point misjudged them.
But, pardon! Pardon is not made for us:
Save, Emperor, it were thine.

Cai.   Whereof there's need:

For 'tis not yours to punish ; ye usurped.

Ye'll have their pardon, or not mine.   Well, Stellio?

    Stell.   I would not vex them even with my pardon,

But, Cæsar bidding, I give it, and goodwill.

    Cai.   And now, Æonia.

    Æon.   I obey, and pardon.

    Cai.   Give him your hands in amity.

    Stell.   Æmilia,

Thy hand ; I'll take it for the children's sake.

    Æmil. [*gives him her hand*].   I have learned thou art less
    faulty than thou seemdst,

And guiltless of her dying.

    Stell. [*to Quintus and Marcus who give him their hands*].
                       Thanks for this.

Your little kinsfolk, whom, from this day forth,

I'll cherish tenfold, shall in love repay you.

    Æon. [*to Æmilia*].   No, Madam ; peace between us, but not
    friendship.

I will not take thy hand, nor [*to Quintus and Marcus*] thine, nor
    thine.

There is no wrong that I could ever do ye,

But you've outmeasured it to me.   We are strangers.

    Cai.   Well, follow thy mood ; we'll smooth thee by and by.

Chafe not, Æmilia ; she's been roughly taxed :

Enough that she has pardoned thee.   Now you,

Brawlers and gapers, and my very good friends,

You've had some sport, eh?   We've been players to you.

Well, you have heard : but understand your ears.

You heard the immaculate worth of chaste Æonia—
Lælia's fast friend—of this unblemished Stellio—
Lælia's most tender lover and true spouse—
You heard how Lælia died alone, untouched ;
You heard these righteous folk, so foul aspersed,
Grant pardon to their penitent accusers.
Was it so?

    Voices [confusedly].   Aye, aye.   Sure, darling Caius.   Eh?
Why does he ask us?   Think, though, had we killed them,
So blameless as they are !   Blessings upon them !

    A voice.   Why doctrinate us over with the tale ?
We have brains behind the ears and eyes, sweet Caius.

                            [Voices assent laughingly.

    Cai.   Good news, my pets.   But go on keeping dark :
Your lords, to borrow the brains, might crack your skulls.

                            [Laughter among the throng.

Depart.   And, if you *must* vent gossiping,
Talk it aright, as your eyes and ears have learned.
And—mark now—whosoever after this
Repeats that lie Lælia was done to death,
Hints of it, thinks it, dreams of it, listens to it,
Shall die.

    Shouts of.   Hail Caius !   Long live Caius Cæsar !

    Cai.   Go ; go, I told ye.   Hail to ye, and good-bye.

              [The throng begins to disperse and go.

You, servants, quick !   Your lady and young lords,
Who presently will start for Formiæ,

Need all prepared in haste.   Fishermen, heigh !

[*Exeunt attendants.*

Keep up the search amain.   Drag the whole bay.

Fishers.   Aye, aye ; that will we.

A fisher.   But there's no whit hope ;
Current and tide beat seaward strong.

Cai.   Go try.

[*To Neda*]   Woman, wast thou not Lælia's?

Neda.   No, my lord ;
Æónia's freedwoman.

Cai.   No matter whose :
Find Lælia's nurses ; bid them, with despatch,
Make ready for the children's going hence.

Stell.   Whither, my lord ?

Cai.   They'll have Æmilia's care.
Memnon, go hurry those.

[*Pauses till the last of the throng have disappeared.*

Friends, I have thought.

This scandal shall be crushed in the birth hour.   Thus :
Thou, Stellio, canst not seemly tarry here ;
Thou'lt come with me.

Stell.   I am thankful.

Cai.   Good.   But whither ?
Thou hast not guessed.   To Æmilia—to *her* mother's.
We all set forth anon for Formiæ.
What ?   Does Æmilia start ?   Inhospitable !
Wilt thou not make me room for three poor days ?

Æmil.   Willing and proudly, Caius ; that thou knowst.

Cai.   And, naturally, Stellio, who's thy son,
Flies to thy roof, like a dove out of the storm,
For cherishing and shelter.

    Stell.   Must I so?
'Twill tax Æmilia.   For, perceive, dear Caius,
She'll need all guest-rooms for thy gracious visit ;
She could not house me.

    Cai.   Tush !   House with her dogs.
Why, Stellio, wilt thou not be spared from scandal ?
Not spare Æonia's honour, meshed with thine ?
I bid thee to Æmilia's for that cause ;
I.   Come, Æmilia ; Lælii, come.   Look down ;
The grounds are thick with waiters for our passing.
We'll thread among them.   [*To Æonia*] Lady, fare thee well :
Fonteia, too.   Thy hand, Æmilia ; come. [*Leads Æmilia.*
Stellio, thou'lt follow us closely with thy brothers :
From time to time lean forward to Æmilia,
Whisper familiarly.

    Stell.   Farewell, Æonia.
Forgive me that my fate has——

    Caius interrupts calling at the exit.   Stellio, we wait.
Lælii, show brotherly with him : make amends.

                    [*Exeunt all but Æonia and Fonteia.*

    Font.   I'm still half dead with fright.   Dear, dear, Æonia !
    Æonia sinks into a seat.

    Font.   Lean upon me, dear.   So.   Thou hast been hard tried.
But, oh, how brave thou stoodst !

Æonia.   I did not hate her.

[*Hides her face in her hands and burst into passionate weeping.*

CHANT FROM THE SHORE.

Gods of our bay, grant our desire,
Send the poor corse to earth and the fire.
Dead one, leave the sea-foam :
Come; come home ; come home.

END OF ACT II.

ACT III.

SCENE I. *Æonia's house at Rome. A sitting-room formed by curtains and a portion of a large interior colonnade. ÆONIA sitting in a musing attitude with a garland on her lap.* NEDA *folding a bridal veil.*

Voice without. May I come in?

Enter FONTEIA.

Font.   I've seen all fitly perfect,
Come look.

Æon.   I'll trust thy ordering. Thou, come rest.

Font.   But the verbenas for the wedding wreath :
'Tis time the bride should gather them.

Æon.   I have.
And, look, the wreath is made.

Font.   Nay, that's too soon :
The leaves may parch in the hours before 'tis worn.

Neda.   Trust me they shall be fresh. [*To Æonia*] May I take
    it now?

Font.   But let me see it tried.

Æon. [*to Neda*].   Well, try it again.
[*To Fonteia*].   I like it well.

Font.   Like it ! good Madam bride !
I know thou dost.   Could it be made of burrs,
Of ominous nightshade, or of rank-breathed leeks,
Thou'ldst think it exquisite, being worn for Stellio.
Come, own it ; own.   Neda, that spray's too high.

    Æon.   I'll own that, being as it is, 'tis fragrant.

    Font.   Aye, that's Love's breath in it. [*To Neda*] Try it with
    the veil.

There !   Stay, that's crooked.   Lovely ! [*To Neda*] Set it so.

Enter LYDIA.

    Æon.   Lydia, why art thou come uncalled?

    Lyd.   Forgive :
'Twas Stellio sent me.   He desires to see thee.

    Æon.   Go bring him.   [*Exit Lydia.*]   [*To Neda*] Take these
    off.   Quick, ere he comes !

    Font.   Nay, let him look.

    Æon.   I shall seem happy foolish.

Enter STELLIO.

Caught !

    Stell.   At a gracious crime, then.   Oh, thou'rt fair !
Is that the very wreath, love ?

    Æon.   Dost thou like it?
For then it is.   Else shall they weave another :
There's time still.

    Stell.   Not another.   This beseems thee.
The mellow golden droopings of the veil,

How they beseem thee too ! Dear veil, dear wreath ;
Dear signs that thou'lt this evening come to home,
To me.

 Font. [*to Neda*]. Now take them off, and put them safe.

 Æon. Why hast thou sought me, Stellio?

 Stell.   Is it wrong ?

The morning wears so slowly to our time :
And I felt a need to see thee. I'll go now.

 Æon. Not yet. Being here, stay now a little while.

 Font. Take care. Thou dost so cosset all his whims,
Thou'lt have a tasking husband of him.

 Æon.   Shall I ? [*Gives Stellio her hand.*

 Stell. [*To Fonteia*]. Thou see'st how much she fears.

 Font.   But, Stellio, say—

Thou hast forgotten to send us word—the Lælii ?
We have kept places ; they'll not come though ?

 Stell.   Yes.

To all ; to the banquet here, the signatures ;
The bride's escorting home, the rites, the supper.

 Font. But not Æmilia ?

. *Stell.*   She'll be here.

 Æon.   She will !

 Stell. To my mind Caius well might have excused them.

 Font. 'Tis their own fault, for what they did at Baiæ.

 Æon. Oh, hush on that.

 Font.   Well but, for very shame,

The wrong she then did now should tie her tongue.
Who's she to chafe if Stellio marries thee,
To scold at Caius for it ?

Stell.   But, dear friend,
Take not the thought that that's because of—Baiæ.
'Tis not.

Font.   Of course 'tis not.   Oh, they ne'er breathe it,
She nor her sons; they're far too well ashamed.
'Tis jealousy of thy clipped widowhood,
And that this union misallies thy first.
I told her plain (owe me no grudge for it, Stellio)
The answer Rome gives *that*, behind her back,
"That thou'lt wed over low; but the bride lower,
She who, far more than ever Æmilia's child,
Could pick her choice of golden bachelors."

Æon.   And I have chosen him whom to have chosen
Will make me prouder than the haughtiest name.

Stell.   And that thou hast chosen me shall be my spur
To higher than my fortunes, worthier thee.

Font.   Now, be the words right auguries.   I'll leave ye:
But, prithee, Stellio, tarry not too long;
'Twould be strange luck if you two were belated; ....
The bride and bridegroom lacking from the wedding !

                              [*Exit Fonteia.*

Æon.   We've time to linger, though.   And, love, 'tis strange,
I am not eager now: I'd, if I could,
Stay the swift moments, waiting peaceful thus.

Stell.   Not I.   And yet I would, though I would not.
We are like bathers bent upon the plunge
And yet a moment dallying, pleased with fears,
Tasting the freshness coyly: then——

                    Re-enter FONTEIA, *hastily.*

Font.   Here's Caius !

Æon.   Caius now !

Stell.   Here?

Font.   I guess not what it means.
He is here in state, at hand, in this corridor,
A crowd behind him.

Enter NEDA.

Neda.   Madam, the emperor's here.
He asked where Stellio was, where thou : he comes.

Æon.   In anger, Neda ?

Neda.   Oh, no ; sure no anger :
He breaks in laughters.   'Tis some good surprise.

[*The curtains are thrown back in haste, from the outside, by
  Slaves of Æonia's, and there is seen a splendid banquet-hall
  surrounded by a colonnade of which the enclosed sitting-room
  is a portion.*

Enter a procession of Priests, Boys, *and* Maidens, *wearing
  chaplets ;* Guards, Musicians ; *amid the procession,* NIGER.
  Then enter CAIUS CÆSAR *in imperial robes, attended by*
  Lictors, State Retinue, Guards, *and* Others.   Mob *following.*

Cai.   Stellio, 'tis thou I seek.   This is thy day :
The mounting sun that has the hours in leash
Is thy bright minister—seems he not ?—thy convoy,
To bring that hour whose pretty name's now Hope
But soon Fulfilment—thy fair marriage-hour,

But he moves tardier than thy dial counts :
Fond loverling, why, thou'rt half a life too soon !

Stell.   If, my good lord, the interval's so long,
'Twere folly not to while some part away :
'Tis wisdom's self thou'rt mocking.

Cai.   That may be.
Wisdom aŋd folly are such natural twins
Their differing mark is one proves fortunate :
And then we know 'twas wisdom : else 'twere the twin.
But come, we wait thee.

Stell.   Wait me !   Whither to go ?

Cai.   To pay thine homage to wronged Jupiter
This day, that's thine, acquits a pious debt.

Stell.   Does it ?   I'm in the dark.

Cai.   Blaspheme not, friend,
Thou knowest there was a dedicating vow ;
Lives pledged to Jove; thy kinsman Niger's one.
Leave jests ; be reverent.

Niger [*to Stellio*].   I am to die.

Stell.   He is to die !   Oh, but this is not earnest.
A kind of masking is it not ?   A pageant ?
A trial of my credulousness?   I see :
I'm to be mocked a little.

Cai.   Hast thou done ?
Be grave now, as beseems ; and take thy place.

Nig. [*to Stellio*]. By me.   And we'll keep up each other's
      hearts.
Thou hast no long loss of me, nor I of life,

I being so far in years.   And, reasoning,
The issue's fair enough ; we should abide it :
For when, in the fever, Caius lay past hope,
And I, 'mid the rest, with dedicating vows,
Devolved our lives his ransom at Jove's will,
I gave the bond deliberate.   Now 'tis claimed.

   Stell.   Gods !   By what sign.

   Cai.   By righteousness and my will.
Shall I see Jove defrauded of his tribute ?
.Then might *he* smile on sacrilege to *me.*
He has been mocked : and I.   A debt for me,
Lives due for mine and not a one yet paid !
Shall the world's prince be bankrupt to Heaven's prince ?
Cease such a stain on Rome !

   Nig.   I'm ready, Caius.

   Cai.   I praise thee there.   But Stellio pulls a lip.
Why, bridegroom, I have thought of thee in all :
Niger's so near in blood, so linked with thee,
So dear, that his atoning is half thine.
Count thyself part in the sacrificial gift,
And the rite a god-sent prelude to thy wedding.

   Nig.   Well, though thy piety's past my desire,
I thank it, Caius, there.   Those were good words.
Nephew, snatch prosperous blessings by my death :
Make a fair omen of it.

   Stell.   'Tis past thought !
Caius, thou canst not bid this old man die ;
Thou wilt not harm the kind grey head Jove spares.

7

What has he done, that never did a crime?
He loved thee, wept, as a father for his son,
To see thy young life go; and then he prayed.
And must he die for that?

 Cai.   His life is Jove's.

 Stell. Jove's and not thine, Lord Cæsar. Touch him not,
Lest Jove avenge....and men.

 Cai. [*laughs*].   Ha! ha! A threat?

Thou'rt merry, bridegroom. [*To the procession*] Come, form file,
 form file:

We spend vain time in chatter. [*To Stellio*] Take thy place [*Points.*

 Stell. [*kneels*]. If thou have pity in thee——

 Cai. [*interrupts*].   I have not.

Godlike authority sees all too well,
And from too far, for pity. We avenge.
Crouch not to me with men's compassionate pleas:
I have outgrown their sense, forgotten it quite.
I'd an inkling of it yet some while far back;
I could have pitied something then—what was it?
A girl, I think—Ah, yes, I have it, thy Lælia.

 Stell. She—Thou—I——[*Pauses confused*].

 Cai.   Why, man, thou art choked with pronouns.
[*To the procession*] Now raise the chorus. March.

 Stell.   Hear me a word.
Spare him, in Lælia's name. She loved him much—
Most daughterly—used him, leaned upon his counsels.

 Cai. Therefore I'll send him to her. To thy place.

 Nig. Prithee, kind nephew, lend me company.

I'll count that better service, more to use,

Than to be kept here lingering through these parleys.

[*Stellio goes to him*] Thanks, thanks, dear boy. Caius, *who*

lingers now ?

Font. [*aside to Æonia*]. He gazes on thee ; speak.

Æon. [*aside to Fonteia*].   I wait his will.

Cai. Æonia, thou hast said no word.

Æon.   I feared.

Cai. And wherefore feared ? And what ?

Æoni.   Omnipotent prince,

I would have been thy suppliant for that life,

That weak poor life so nought before thy power,

I would have prayed with Stellio, but I feared—

Not for myself; I'd dare, for Stellio's kinsman,

Confront thine anger. No ; but oftentimes

Unauthorized and too presumptuous lips

By their misliked concordance spoil that suit

A better suitor, left unhelped, might win.

But now thou hast given me speech. Oh Caius, Master,

Grant me for Stellio this slight easy boon—

A little thing for thee, a worthless thing—

Just one old man's worn life. Oh think, one word,

One only breath of thine, "Live," or else "Perish,"

And on that breath hangs a man's agony.

Say "Live." Be it "Live," great Caius. Look, he's old.

On, on my wedding-day spare Stellio this !

Cai. Thy beauty is as marvellous as they say :

More than I thought. Thou'rt goddess-beautiful.

I'm sorry, for thy beauty's sake.   Thou hast failed.

The thing I have decreed will be.   Priests, on.

    Nig.   Farewell, my nephew's bride.   Joy to the wedding.

    Æon.   Heaven send thee back to it yet, I pray.   Farewell.

[*Exeunt Niger and Stellio with the procession of Priests, Boys,
    and Maidens moving to music.*

    Cai.   Well, lovely lady, we're to meet anon.

    Æon.   I'm proud thou'lt do our nuptials so much grace.

Stellio and I once owed thee life, acquittal ;

Now, by thy help and honouring countenance,

Almost our union....all its safety.   Thanks.

    Cai.   Thou yet shalt thank me more, divine Æonia.

Good-bye, awhile. [*Exit joining in the procession. Exeunt
    following him Officers of his State Retinue, Attendants,
    Lictors, Guards, &c., and Mob.*

    Æon. [*to Neda*].   Run, see which way they take.

And send me forth a slave or two—swift-footed—

Tell them to bring quick news of any chance.

    Font.   Be sure he'll never send him to the death.

    Æon.   I am sure he will.   Didst thou not note his voice,

Its quiet sure intent ; not note his mien,

Smiling with safe command ?   He has in him

The self-assured resolve of perfect power.

He has seen his meaning, and he'll carry it.

Niger was tedious ; but poor soul !   And Stellio !

    Font.   Thou'lt comfort him.

    Æno.   I hope it.

Re-enter NEDA.

Well, which way ?

Neda.   By the road to the Capitol.

Æon.   'Tis even so.

We'll see them for a while from the upper rooms.

[*Exeunt omnes.*

ACT III.

Enter MEMNON, NEDA, ÆONIA'S STEWARD, *and several* Servants, *who begin arranging the hall for a banquet.*

Steward. This is the chamber Caius saw.

Memn.   Yes this.

Stew. But he's not seen our winter banquet hall.
'Tis for true space as large—well-nigh as large—
For this portico and the bays help nought for meals—
'Tis an easier shape for serving, properer far—
A straight plain oblong, and the walls well seen ;
And, 'tis a secret, but those walls are walls !
Æonia's had new frescoes—such a price !—
Penelope's nuptials, Thetis's, and Psyche's,
And Hercules with Hebe 'mid the gods—
So near the kitchen too !

Memn.   Oh loss ! Oh climax !

Neda. But truly 'tis a pity, though thou laugh.
And the other hall's prepared.

Stew.   A very show !
All trim, all decked, all laid, save but the meats.
And Caius asks for *this* hall !

Memn.   'Tis his way.

This chamber takes his fancy—that's not strange ;

'Tis of a noble plan.

    Stew.   'Tis not the other.

    Neda. Well, well, 'tis where the banquet is to be :

Nor is Æonia vexed.   Old grumbler, peace :

Art Roman and wilt grudge to pleasure Caius ?

    Stew. I'll do it, I'll do it.   But if he had seen the——[*shouts*

    to some slaves who are dragging a couch clumsily] Ah !

Is that your plan ? You'll break the foot ! To the left !

                                            [*Goes to them.*

    Memn. [*to Neda*]. I need some words with thee more pri-
vately.

    Neda. No, no ; we have no secrets, thou and I.

    Memn. That means thou'rt fain to have my open love.

Eh, Neda ?

    Neda. Means I'll have nor love nor lies.

Eh, Memnon ?

    Memn.   Prithee hear me more apart.

'Tis something grave.   Find us a quiet place.

    Neda. That will I not, and be the house's mock;

[*To a slave who passes near*]. To draw the curtains, is it ?

    Slave.   There's no need.

    Neda. I'll help thee.   Pull that cord.

    [*Curtains between the pillars close and shut off the rest*

        of the hall as in the opening of last scene.

                         This is our won't.

See, this embrasure's now a singled room :

And, sheltered thus, Æonia sits here often.
'Tis ready for her now.

Memn.   I see.   We're in it.
But can they hear?

Neda.   Can they!   Away so far,
And in that stir!   Or would some fool, dost think,
Ply ear at the curtain, visible?   My faith!
Although our lady's no hard punisher,
There'd be a ear at stake for that.

Memn.   Listen—Nearer.

Neda.   No; say it where we stand.

Memn.   Well : since we're safe——
Thou'rt sure of that?—I'm a love messenger.

Neda.   Messenger?

Memn.   Only that.   And not to thee.

Neda.   Prithee, good sir, waste not my time in follies :
My mistress needs me.   And, for my own part,
I am not wont to chatter alone with men.

Memn.   Swear—but no need : the secret's, in itself,
So perilous thou'lt keep it for life's sake.

Neda.   What?   Tell me.   Wilt thou?

Memn.   Caius loves Æonia.

Neda.   Caius!   Since when?

Memn.   'Twas news to me just now.
[*Muses*] When *did* it grow in that strange brain of his?
Just now?   Or when he first set eyes on her?
Or in that coil at Baiæ?   Or this morning?
Well, well. [*To Neda*] Neda, thou question'st me, "Since when?"

'Tis sure enough that more of his most trust
Than Caius gives another he gives me :
Then, if I know the answer, 'tis his secret ;
If I know not, 'tis even more his secret ;
Therefore I must not tell thee.

Neda.   But—'tis true?

Memn.   It should be true, since he will marry her.

Neda.   But that's impossible.

Memn.   Is there new law?

Neda.   Oh, I'll not heed thee more : 'tis fooling, all.

Memn.   Heed carefully, and remember. 'Tis strange earnest.
Caius, that has no child, is widower long;
'Tis the second autumn now since Junia died,
And that was March.   Caius desires remarriage.
The people urge him too.

Neda.   But why Æonia?

Memn. [*aside*]. And why Æonia, truly? Save he's mad.
[*To Neda*] Note, Neda, if she doubt his sure intent,
That Caius says, and laughs at talk of fitness,
To please him's best nobility there is,
The sole that any woman could bring *him.*
All being to him in one disparity.

Neda.   None less, then, all being least.

Memn.   .   Take this too, Neda,
The wife of Caius has no former rank,
Greater or less being all too small for her.

Neda.   I'd say so, were I he, and choose at will.

Memn.   Now, that Æonia is to-day a bride

Makes her meet prize for him, who, not by leave
And not by common wooing, should take wife,
But swooping on her, as Romulus took Hersilia,
And as Augustus Livia.   I have told thee.

Neda.   I marvelled how, as rapt, he gazed upon her.
Yet, marry her !   And he refused her prayer.

Memn.   He will, in two clear hours from now, be here.
Not openly yet, but to concert their course.
Neda, beware.   Breathe nothing save to herself.
Caius has trusted thee.   What thou must do—
For which there'll be sure brave reward—is small :
Thou'lt on some pretext, in two hours from now,
Be at the outer gate in watch for Caius,
And lead him to her least observed thou canst.
Meanwhile, go tell her ; and, if she hold back,
Persuade her to her fortune.

Neda.   *That* I dare not.
Repeat thy tidings....yes, that's my plain duty :
Convoy him....well, she'll sure depute me that :
But, thrust my tattle on her in such case !

Memn.   Why, she's not cruel.

Neda.   But she'd awe me down.
And, Memnon, dost thou dream she'll leave her Stellio?
She'd die first ; that she would.

Stell. [*without*].   May I come, Æonia ?

Enter STELLIO.

Stell.   Where is thy lady, Neda ? [*Throws himself on a seat.*

Neda.   I'll go see.

Memn. [*to Neda*]. Note; in two hours will the emperor's
   gardener

Bring to Æonia freshly gathered apples.

[*To Stellio*]. My salutations.   [*Exit Memnon.*

Stell.   Child, go tell Æonia

That I——

Enter ÆONIA.

Æon.   I heard thy voice in the corridor.

Stell.   I knew thou'dst let me see thee.

Æon.   Surely that.

Thou hast brought thy grief to me.

Neda.   Madam, may I go?

Æon.   Do, my good girl : and take this to Fonteia—

[*to Stellio*] The clasp, my Stellio, with our names in one.

[*to Neda*] Say 'tis a record token of to-day,

To keep for sake of us—the date's upon it ;

Pray her to wear our gift.   [*Exit Neda.*

Stell.   Niger is dead.

Æon.   I know it.   Dear, he'll be *my* kinsman soon ;

We both will mourn him, both, with every due,

Honour his memory.

Stell.   The dear old man !

So calm.   Didst hear the manner of his death?

Hurled from the rocks.   They led him——

Æon.   I have heard it :

I had a messenger.   Think other thoughts ;

Sorrow should wait our leisure.   Niger sleeps ;
And is there no one living claims to-day ?
Thou hast thy wife. . . . Æonia.

 Stell.   Thou art all.

 Æon. Then, if thou dost so love me, with such hope,
Smile not so forced and sadly—not to-day.
"Joy to the wedding" that was his farewell.

 Stell. And he bequeathed his death for fortunate omen.
But—ah, my sweet, thou hast a valorous heart,
Now, beside thee, warmed with thy words, thy smile,
I once more know we are happy, must be happy—
'Tis our right who love so much : but this strange ill,
So great a grief, so sudden ! and then, so strange !
Done in Heaven's name as though Jove's self had struck me !
I am turned weak, and, in my will's despite,
Remember her whom we must not remember.

 Æon. Will thy repenting, that wrongs *me*, serve *her*?
Would *my* repenting, that were wrong to thee ?
For my sake put that memory away,
As I for thine.   What price we paid, my Stellio,
Is paid ; and if it were too great, is paid.
Come out from the past with me.   We have no past :
Our life's new found.

 Stell.   'Tis so : we have new found life.
What once I took for happiness was slumber.

 Æon. Think, then, that, as, in moments while sleep breaks
And yet 'tis not full waking, ill dreams come,
So dreams to us, and so shall end forgotten.   .

Stell.   Thou art my life, I thine : I'll think but that.

Æon.   Thou hast promised it : but that.   No grief to-day.

Stell.   Well, I'll come back all happy.   I should go.
Yet, need I go so soon ?

Æon.   Invader, yes.
And there's to do still.   Caius has a fancy,
Sends word 'twill much fit his theatric sense
If the feast is held in the arcaded hall.

Stell.   'Tis like him.   Nought so real but's his show,
And everywhere's his stage.   Oh, and there's more :
He's bent on joyaunce—This I should have told thee,
But it slipped my mind—that when, at Niger's gate,
He let me leave his train—For he's still forth,
Pacing in slow procession through the rabble ;
Himself he blazons them his zealot deed,
" Thank me : " he cries, " God Jupiter has his toll : "
And they that not a knave but would, if he could,
Steal Jupiter's last doit for wine and lusts,
Howl bigotries, call him " Champion of the gods "
And range themselves on the side of injured Heaven.

Æon.   They'd be as readily impious if he pleased.
Let it not chafe thee ; 'tis no shame to Niger :
Acclaiming Caius's stern sacrifice
They mind not of the victim....whom, be sure,
They'll sigh upon in a to-morrow's tale.
But what is it thou shouldst tell me ?

Stell.   Oh, the message.
Caius sends mimes : they'll dance a piece of his.

Æon. I have goodly music hired, and Lydia's lyre.
Better to have all costly seemliness
But nought of pageant. Well ; his way must be.
And twill while the banquet through the easier.

    Stell. I would the day were through, and we in peace.

    Æon. So I : and the next days too, till, love, ere long,
We'll win ourselves away, as thou hast planned,
To dear repose apart, and nurse our joy
In thy lone farm in the hushed unpeopled hills.

    Stell. Oh for that moment ! Rest, ineffable rest !
Stillness, with thee ! We'll, like two truant children,
Make festival of but to walk or speak,
Of every common chance, of every turn,
All sights, all sounds, all momentary nothings,
All trackless vacant hours, all dreamful pause,
Because they're ours....our secret and our own.
Good-bye, wife, one once more : then, no good-byes.

    Æon. Good-bye awhile, till soon.   [*Exit Stellio.*

    Æon.   Life will be good.
He shall never love me less ; I'll keep him, keep him !
My love, thou art mine : I will not have for long
So much of rival as one pale regret.

Re-enter NEDA.

    Neda. Madam, I've news.

    Æon.   Is there need that I should hear?
Canst thou not deal with it ?

    Neda.   No. Oh, 'tis secret !

Æon. Dost thou therefore burn to tell it?

Neda.   Oh, dear lady,

'Tis a high matter—maybe dangerous.

Memnon has told me : and 'tis positive :

Our Caius is impassioned in thy love,

Argues, with scores of reasons and desires,

No Roman dame's so fit to be his spouse.

Æon. Woman, *what?*

Neda.   I have written it—word by word--

Lest a jot might slip my mind waiting to tell thee—

The very every words.

Æon.   Give it me.

Neda.   This.   [*Gives a paper.*

I know by Memnon's way 'tis sure plain truth.

Æon. [*reading*]. " The wife of Caius has no former rank,

Greater or less being all too small for her."

                    [*Drops the paper on her lap.*

Neda. There's over leaf. [*aside*] The news has fairly stunned
    her.

Æon. Neda, since when? Did Memnon tell thee when?

Neda. Caius's trust is——

Æon. [*interrupts*].   When? I asked thee when?

Neda. Memnon was doubtful when the thought began :

Perchance when Caius first set eyes on thee.

Æon. No; no; it cannot be he thought it then,

In Rome, ere Baiæ. I am sure 'tis new.

Neda. And Memnon said it might be new to-day.

Æon. Doubtless. 'Tis that. Just a new whim to-day.

I trust 'twill pass as soon, being so useless.

Neda. But he's resolute to wed thee.

Æon. Now thou'rt blundering.

Memnon did never think to tell thee that :

Since 'tis impossible now.

Neda. He answered that.

Thou hast not read what's on the other side.

Æon. I saw it not. [*reads*] .... "and as Augustus Livia."

Livia ! [*To Neda*] Well, Neda, first we'll make safe shreds.

[*Tears the paper carefully.*

Next : be in watch, as bid, when Caius comes ;

Thou'lt say I have no privacy to see him,

Being (as I will be) 'mid a flock of women,

Donning my wedding robes. If he ask further—

Though wisely he'll take that for what I mean—

But if he question plainly, then say thus :

" Æonia thanks her prince for so great honour,

But ill would merit that high gift he named

If, even for *its* sake, she were perjurer ;

Therefore she prays him favour his own work,

That contract she now cannot break ; nor would."

Neda. Yet think——

Æon. [*interrupts*]. All thou canst bid me think I know—

Know as thou canst not feel it. Greatness—power—

The strong delight of them....foregone ! Then, dangers—

If Caius be not pacified, and bear grudge—

Dangers to both of us. But that's *perchance :*

And I'd front that with Stellio, he with me,

But not that we should lose each other now ;
Not falseness, ignominy to myself, to him ;
No, nor that we should hate each other, Stellio.

   Neda. I meant not that.

   Æon.   Belike thou didst not, Neda
I had forgotten I talked to thee.   But, speak :
What's in thy big eyes' gaze ?

   Neda.   I thought perchance—
If thou wilt gainsay him—thyself shouldst say it ;
Not thy mere handmaid.   Even a letter written—
I speak but loving thee, of care for thee.

   Æon. I know thee, Neda : thou *dost* speak by love.
And maybe thou sayst wisely.   I'll yet think.
Come to me ere 'tis time to watch for Caius.   [*Exit Æonia.*

   Neda. I knew she'd never yield to even *that* bait.
If ever there was love 'tis hers for Stellio.
But, oh, I fear !   Caius scarce is what he was.   ·   [*Exit.*

ACT III.

SCENE III. *The same curtained embrasure of the colonnade of the Banquet Hall in Æonia's house.*

ÆONIA, *seated.*

Neda [*without*]. This way, good gardener; this way with thy apples.

Enter through the curtains CAIUS *in a country servant's dress and a cloak; and* NEDA.

Neda. Will it please thee sit. I'll quick go call Æonia.
Æon. [*comes forward*]. I am here already. Neda, go my girl.
                                      [*Exit Neda.*
Cæsar, I will obey thee.
   Cai.   Is it so?
Thy handmaid, when I forced her chary tongue,
Deemed thou'dst be recusant.
   Æon.   I have thought much.
I am ambitious, Caius.
   Cai.   Beauty can be.
   Æon. I will not feign. I did decide averse:
For I love Stellio. But since....I have reasoned.
Caius, thou art our lord, power's very self:
Am I to be thy consort.

Cai.   I have said it.

What ! Does Æonia think I woo her shame ?

Æon. No. Have I not averred I will obey thee ?

Cai. Dost love me ?

Æon.   I revere the Emperor.

Cai. Art glad to marry me ?

Æon.   No, I am not glad.

But proud....as if I were made queen in Heaven.

Cai. Pity we met not sooner.

Æon.   Would we had !

Cai. And so friend Stellio is the sufferer.

Aye, dost thou wince ?

Æon.   Thy consort will be thine.

Cai. But thou *dost* love him.

Æon.   I'll not tell thee no.

[*impatiently*] Why, leave me to him if thou wilt. I love him.

Cai. The better. For thou'lt hound him from thee ; Eh ?

Æon. What thy wife *should* do will I do ; no else.

Cai. That's much ; if my wife's fit for me....as thou art.

No answer, sweetling ?

Æon.   I know nought to add.

And rather would I learn what's now thy hest :

For the wedding hour draws nigh.

Cai.   How shall we do ?

Æon. Thou shouldst command. I have no counsel ready :

I can but take thy will.

Cai.   Oh, but we'll choose.

Now, what's thy plan how to dispose of Stellio ?

Æon.   But to be traitor to him : to thee faithful.

Cai.   Good.   Traitor to him.   But the way of the trick ?
Come to plain business : what's our Stellio's fate?

Æon.   Thou wouldst not harm him !

Cai.   Startled art thou, poppet ?
Thy chestnuts cast into the braize to roast,
Then " Oh, they'll be hot and bite my finger-tips ! "
Prithee take not thy needs so gingerly.
Now : Stellio's spirity ; he might snarl complaints,
Snap at his masters, even—me and thee ;
He could din us deaf before we'd muzzled him.
'Twould spoil our honeymoon.   That sets thee thinking.

Æon.   I fear, in sooth, some passion in his hurt.
Thou hast, most sure, no loyaller friend than he,
And, showed he fierce or sullen, being so used,
Thou couldst not count it to his blame.   He's loyal.
But, lest his grief pass measure the first while,
Remove him to some post—a worthy post—
In a far province.

Cai.   Little isles are safest.

Æon.   That's banishment—prison—disgrace.   Whence that
to him ?

Cai.   So warm, my chick ?   See that I grow not jealous.
Well, banish him with alms of place and pay,
The way thou sayst, and get him far enough.
That's now thy project.   'Tis good prudence, too :
For, though reproach were dumb upon his lips,
Yet would his presence nip thy joy in greatness,

Shrivelling thy heart like breath of a haunting ghost.

Æon. Ah !

Cai. And thou'dst in all he did, or missed to do,
Find memories and imagined scorn or hate.
Yes, yes, we'll have thee rid of him.   But—own it—
Thy mind's yet chary for this cast-off spouse :
Thou'lt hustle him forth away ; aye, but there's this,
That's forth from rushing in the lion's jaws,
From rousing me.   Thou hast a care for that.

Æon. I have a care for that.   Do thou so too.
Thine honour needs him safe....*our* honour, Caius.

Cai. I need him dead.   So thou dost.

Æon.   Stellio dead !

Cai. Shiver at that !   Why, wherefore should he live ?
Thou hast done with him.   Come, face thy need, my pretty :
Thou'dst have our Romans crouch to thee and adore,
But scarce wert fain of scurrilous jests for tag,
And " Look, sirs, look, there's he could tell us tales,
August Æonia's Stellio.   What, not know him ?
A stranger, sir, in Rome ? "   Then comes thy story.

Æon. Speak no more of our marriage ; it being thus.
And yet they honoured Livia.

Cai.   Livia, chick ?
Yes, Livia.   Woman ne'er had place like hers....
Till thou thyself.   I knew thou'dst muse on Livia.
And 'twas no bridegroom but her goodman husband—
Progeny with them too, born and unborn—
When Livia's emperor took her, as thine thee.
If Livia was revered why not thou more ?

Æon.   I will be.   'Twas my thought.

Cai.   Aye, but there's this ;

Livia, my honey poppet, had no secrets ;

The man she left, if he had raved with spite,

Had never a spite to rave for news to Rome—

Just a plain husband, came by her honestly ;

No tales for *him* to tell.

Æon.   Thou dost not think—

Thou dost not dare to think me wanton.

Cai.   Tush !

Not wanton, chick ; not Stellio's light o' love :

No, no.   There's short of that, and there's worse than that,

And there's not being that ; and that thou art not

Content thee, for I know thee.   But, at Baiæ,

He was thy suitor ; therefore Lælia....fell.

Æon.   Thyself art witness of our innocence :

Thou sawst her fall.

Cai.   I saw her leap in the sea.

Listen, Æonia, thou who art my bride,

That girl thy Stellio's treachery slew, I loved.

She was a something tender left my heart—

Tender and sacred like a daisy-weed

Some tired old man finds by his mother's tomb,

Who died while he was young enough for daisies.

I have forgotten kindliness since she went.

[*Muses*] 'Tis strange—most strange—I could not marry her :

If I had done it, taken her from Stellio, [*muses silently.*

Æon.   I wait thine ending, Caius.

Cai.   Ending? Yes?
My ending? True. Lælia was one to love :
Not beautiful and cruel and strong as thou,
Not fit for me, as thou ; but perfect sweet—
Therefore I could not wed her. But I loved her.
And Stellio's treachery killed her. He's to perish.

Æon. Why dost thou talk of treachery? And what proof?
Who says he was my suitor when she died?
Who but thyself in his fresh widowhood   .
Didst draw his thought to me, then urge our marriage,
And, when we doubted, broke down our delays?

Cai. Make no vain pleadings : Heaven and I know all.
The villain wooed thee, plotted Lælia's death,
And then she knew, and died. I have planned his doom.

Æon. Then plan mine too : I am the guiltier.

Cai. Softly, my pretty. *Thy* fault's loveliness—
Such loveliness as lured his fluttering wits—
Shall I not pardon loveliness in my bride?

Æon. Pardon me nothing, or else pardon him.
That passion thou dost count his crime I shared.

Cai. I'm sure 'twas *his* beginning. *He* marked *thee,*
Ere *thou,* responsive, *him.* He perishes.

Æon. Wilt thou not know? I say then I must perish.
He was my suitor, hast thou said? He was.
I made him bold with answering consent ;
I gave him troth for marriage, were he freed.

Cai. Not thou wast bound ; he sole. *Thou* wast not Lælia's.

Æon. 'Twas I that, reckless, when she stole upon us,

Punished her with the truths she spied to know,
And wrought her jealous panic : I, not Stellio.

    Cai. So ; was it thus ? That's the missed part I knew not.
No matter, for it changes nought I knew.
Æonia, thou as well, with prayers and claims,
Mightst think to win rude Tiber, winding back,
To change the path he has shaped him to his gulf,
As me from my fulfilling. I have willed
Stellio's to die : and as for thee....Well, well.
Good ; resolute hands clasped tight, head back, fixed gaze—
Unflinching mute denial—a good pose.
Keep it, my pretty ; thou canst listen in it.
I grant to Stellio death in a happy cup,
With thee for minister—no worse. Or else—
'Tis vowed to Lælia's ghost, inviolable—
Or else shall he and thou, Rome's hooted scandal,
Make public answer, branded, both, with her death
And thou with ribald shames coarse tongues shall gleek ;
Then infamous you'll part—he to his torture,
The forfeit Rome calls "ancient," killed by whipping ;
Thou to thy torture....ignominious life.
Die with thy jilted spouse, my own betrothed ?
No, no : and he'd scarce thank that last devotion,
Seeing he well should know thy pact with me :
Not die, but live, his farewells in thine ear—
That surely would be curses. Live....and where ?

    Æon. Nowhere for long. I'll die.

    Cai.   No ; thou'lt be watched.

The where I plan for's Pandataria.

A horrible sound to a woman, is it not?

So lone, so desolate, so past all hope.

No lover more, nor friend, nor praising eyes,

No barter of light news, no sights, no feasts,

No times for rich attire to deck her beauty—

And the beauty moulders off; she's old there young.

A dismal goal for a woman, Pandataria—

My mother died there—*Her* name, though, 's unstained.

Women have pined in that island, squalid, scorned,

Entreating in a loathsome penury,

Made the base thing slaves punish or excuse.

I'd shudder at the name, chick, were I thou.

Thou'rt not all blameless, chick; no, not all blameless:

That's why I less need spare a sort of smart—

Secret, though, and thou'lt bear it.   Aye, 'twill smart.

But the best blackberries perch where, reaching them,

One catches on most thorns : pricks pay for fruit.

Note me, dear ; for thou'rt wandering.

    Æon.   I hear all.

    Cai.   We make thee safe from Stellio.   Good : but how?

Not by his open death, lest, having time,

He turn upon thee and bequeath thee scandal.

For this cause too can I not, eagle-like,

Swoop on thee, mine out of his very grasp,

Strong in the face of day.   Didst thou think that?

    Æon.   I thought it was thy thought.

    Cai.   If thou indeed

Wert that white saint thou'dst lief be if thou couldst,
Wert that brave innocence we'll have thee seem,
Such jest I'd have upon him.   'Tis my loss.
But for thy sake—*thy* sake, my proud Æonia—
Our prank must pass in secret ; he must free thee,
As Lælia him, by dying opportune.
Now, here's a phial, chick—Hey ! swoon not, fool.
Where's water ?

    Æon.   I'll not swoon.   I am well.   Thy meaning ?

    Cai.   Mix it in wine.   Fear not, it makes no taste ;
He'll not discover thee.   Give it him anon,
At thy banquet : I'll make signal—just a smile.
Soon he'll be meekly faint, and then.... That's all.
Take the phial [*holds it to her ; she recoils*].   Ah, not ready for
    it yet ? [*sets it on a table beside her.*]
'Tis in thy reach.

    Æon.   Bid *me* destroy him !   Me !
I ask to die with him, since—[*breaks off*].   But thou'rt mad.

    Cai.   Yes, mad enough to govern saner folk.
Why, why, what's talk for now ?   Thou'lt face thy need.
But choose, thyself, your fates.

    Æon.   Oh gods !   Oh gods !

    Cai.   Call on no god save me : 'tis I rule this.

    Æon.   And if I did it—Would thy vengeance end ?

    Cai.   By the strongest oath, by my own sacredness,
I swear that, when thou hast wrought my work on Stellio,
I am thy husband—take my hand on that [*she recoils*].
Thou wilt not ?   Well, I have given it ; 'tis pledged—

Thy husband.... save thyself it were denied me.

Take up thy phial [*she takes it slowly from the table*].   Good.
 Thou'lt do it.

Æon.   No! [*Dashes the phial to shivers on the ground,*
                    and exit.

Cai. [*following her*].   Thou hast still thy choice.   I'll bring
   another phial [*Comes back laughing, takes up his basket of*
   apples, and exit through the curtain where he entered.

ACT III.

SCENE IV. *The same banquet hall in Æonia's house.* STELLIO *and* ÆONIA *at table as Bridegroom and Bride : with them* CAIUS, QUINTUS, MARCUS, ÆMILIA, FONTEIA, *and other* Guests. MEMNON, STEWARD, NEDA, EUTHYMUS, *and various* attendants *and* slaves *serving tables, etc.*, Musicians.

Curtains are thrown back at the upper end of the room and Mime-Actors *perform a Mime-dance representing the sea-god* Glaucus *and* Nereids *alluring a* Girl *who is withheld in vain by* Life, *personified as her lover. Mime-Actors withdraw by the way they came.*

Cai. Well mimed indeed ! Well danced ! What sayst thou, Quintus ?

Quint. Excellent grace.

Marc. 'Twas vividly portrayed.

1*st Guest.* Our mimes will outshine nature soon.

Cai. But soon ? Do they not now ? This pasty's marvellous good.

Stell. 'Twere a fair world if nature made such shows.

Cai. Do ye hear him, friends ? He feigns he saw it ; he ! Oh hypocrite ! Thou sawst but fair Æonia. [*Laughters.*

Stell. Spare blushes, Caius, and my merry friends : Mocking's ill sauce to meat.

Cai.   What ! canst thou feed ?

Æonia, he's no lover.

Æon.   I, my lord?

To my poor mind they danced most exquisitely.   [*Laughters.*

Cai.   We learn love can make deaf as well as blind.

2nd Guest [*Fonteia's husband*].   Some men would wish love
   could make some wives dumb.

Font.   Some wives might wish their husbands shorter ears.
                                            [*Laughters.*

Cai.   Here's to Fonteia's wifely wish. [*drinks*].

2nd Guest.   I thank thee.

Short hearing's armour for a wise man's brain.

3rd Guest.   Dost think the longest ears needs hear the most ?

Cai.   They hold the most : judge for thyself, my Piso.
                                            [*Laughters.*

Quint.   Ne'er mind our laughing, man.

3rd Guest [*Piso*].   Why, I laugh too.

Stell.   We're food for mirth in turn ; but merrily.

'Tis a game of chasing, and the caught may catch.

Cai.   Æmilia wears grave looks.

Æmil.   And a grave heart.

Cai.   Thou shalt see somewhat—mimes to suit thy taste.

[*Calls*] Ho, there !   Dulce !   Come !

Enter from the curtains at the farther end of the room the two
   CHILDREN *of Stellio and Lælia, followed by* Dulce *encour-*
   aging them.   They wear garlands and carry flowers.

Boy [*to Dulce*].   Shall we say it now ? [*Dulce nods.*]

Children [*advance to Æonia*].   Dead Lælia's children greet
  thee, lady bride.

She is not jealous of thee.   Think of her.

Here are feast-day flowers we bring thee for her sake.

> [*They give Æonia flowers: she takes them silently.*

Cai.   'Tis pretty how they do it. [*To the children*] Well,
  what next?

Children [*turn to Stellio*].   Dead Lælia's children greet thee,
  bridegroom father.

She'll be to-day contented.   Think of her.

Here are marriage flowers we give thee in her name.

> [*They give him flowers.*

Stell.   I'll take them for her gift and her forgiveness.

This make good omen, and——[*stops.*]

Cai.   Say on.

Stell.   I thank their innocent voices for it——[*stops*].

Cai.   What?

Stell.   Faint—faint—I——

Cai.   Quick !   Support him hence.

To the portico there. And close the curtaining screen.

He'll come to himself there shortly.

Children.   Oh ! the flowers

Boy.   Father, the flowers.   He has not taken them.

[*Euthymus and others lead Stellio forward and help him on to
  a seat.*

Cai.   Æonia, go thou to him.

> [*Æonia rises slowly and perplexed.*

>   Thou dazed too !

Go to the cooler freshening air with Stellio.

His qualm will pass there soon.

Æon.   Where shall I go?

A servant supporting Stellio.   He's better.

Euth.   Fetch him water.

Cai.   Friends, 'tis nought.

'Twill briefly pass.   We'll not break up the feast.

Keep merry. [*To Æonia*] Come, we'll spare thee to his help.

[*Leads her to Stellio.*]   [*To Euthymus and the others*]   Have
    the curtains drawn I bade ye.

    [*The curtains are drawn, shutting of the rest off the banquet
    hall from the sitting-room portion as in the foregoing scenes*].

Cai. [*to Æonia*].   Stay beside him :

We know thy heart desires it ; and, belike,

Thou'lt best revive him.   Be not scared, dear lady,

'Tis nought. [*Aside to her*] Make better show, the slaves observe
    thee :

Go, bathe his forehead.

[*Æonia takes a handkerchief from Euthymus and bathes Stellio's
                    forehead.*]

Stell.   Oh! I breathe again.

A faintness took me : but it passes.   Dearest !

Æon.   Rest thee ; lean back again.

Euth.   Just few more minutes ;

And then thou'lt be thyself, dear master.

Cai.   Yes.

Euth.   He's strong by wont ; but 'tis a tasking day :

The mind's stir tires the body.

Cai.   Niger's death :
That's somewhat.   Niger had good years to live.
A hale strong man he was, though venerable,
And fain he would have lived.   'Twas a dire death.
But he leaped well.   He'd tears, though ; some.
   Euth.   He's paler.
Fainting again.
   Stell.   No ; better.   Let me be
   Cai.   We'll leave him to thy ministry, Æonia
Bring him back soon, revived :. or, if ye linger,
I'll come to scold ye.   I'll go keep all merry.
Come, fellows, come ; your master needs not you.
[*Exeunt through the curtains Caius, Euthymus, and the others.*
   Stell.   More water.   Thanks, sweet love.
   Æon.   Thou hast not pain ?
   Stellio.   But little—none, I think.   Gaze not so strangely.
Love, be not frightened.   Nay, I am nigh well :
Only my brow throbs somewhat : thou shalt heal me ;
Lay thy cool hand upon it.   Why !   Thou'rt death-cold.
   Æon.   That's useful, then.
   Stell.   Oh, the dear cooling hand !
   Æon.   Ah !
   Stell.   What, dear ?
   Æon.   Hush, hush !   Rest thee.   '
   Stell.   The qualm's gone.
And the throbbings in my head thou hast stilled.   I'm well .
Ready to join the feasters.   But let's wait :
I'm tired : I shall face them better if we wait.

Æon.   Best not go back at all.   Relapse might seize thee.

Stell.   No fear.   My vigour's coming with each breath.
Fear not, sweet darling : talk to me happily,
Heal me my heart of thoughts—Niger—and Lælia—
Fill it with thee ; then we'll go back and laugh.

Æon.   Stellio ! my Stellio !

Stell.   •   *I* must comfort *thee* ?
We are over-strained.   I would to-day were by.

Æon. [aside]. I must.   I can.   'Tis the last mercy left him.
He shall die happy—shall die loving me.
[*To Stellio*].   And when to-day is by, if we love well,
All time will seem too short save when we're parted.

Stell.   *If* we love well ?

Æon.   True, a most obsolete *if.*
Yet a good *if* since it brings back thy smile.

Stell.   Remorse is meaningless with *thee* near, Æonia,
And sorrows pale into my joy of thee,
Like planets overtaken by the dawn.

Æon. [clings to him passionately]. Take me ! Oh take me !
   Hold me to thy heart.
Say thou art happy.   Kiss me.

   [*Peals of laughter from the banqueters within are heard.*]

Stell.   Thou more than life !

            Re-enter CAIUS CÆSAR.

Cai.   How's the dear sufferer, fair Æonia ?   Well ?
Or have our jocund sounds disturbed his head—

                    9

The music and the mirth of his own nuptials?
'Twere pity, that.

> *Æon.*   He's not disturbed.   He's better.

> *Cai.*   Right news : we need him better.

> *Stell.*   I am well :

I'll come.   There's a strange weakness, though.

> *Cai.*   ·   Not strange.

That's how the creeping venom always works,
That she has given thee.

> *Stell.*   Given ?   What hast thou said ?

> *Cai.*   Thou art poisoned.   Understand me : poisoned, man.

Dost know it?

> *Stell.*   Yes, I know it now.   I am poisoned.

> *Cai.*   By her. .... Æonia.

> *Stell.*   No. [*To Æonia*] Dear, hold my hand.

[*To Caius*] Whoso accused her to thee, Caius, lied.

> *Cai.*   Lælia's avenged, and by Æonia's self :

She gave thee poison at the wedding feast.
Thou hast some minutes left to curse her in.
Oh, doubt still : bid her swear she gave no drug.

> *Stell.*   Æonia, darling, speak though there's no need.

They have taken me from thee, love, and, I being gone,
Would blast thee, helpless, with this monstrous charge ;
Dear, answer—not for me—but Cæsar hears ;
Bid him protect thine innocence.

> *Cai.*   Good ! Good ! [*laughs boisterously.*

> *Stell.*   Æonia ?

> *Æon.*   Thou'dst have died by a worse doom.

Stell. 'Tis true? *True?*

Cai.   Prithee, Stellio, yell less sharp,

The company will hear thee ; 'tis not seemly.

And I'll not have thee fright my pretty here ;

She did it for no spite, but reasonably.

Thou'rt in the way, man, rubbish in her way ;

She had need to rid herself to marry me.

Aye, gaze from one to the other, gasp and choke ;

Æonia's mine, my pretty one, my pet.

> [*Strokes Æonia's head and pats her cheek.   She shrinks but
> stands still.*]

Oh, she's so fain to be another Livia !

That's her sweet way of talk.   Wish my wife joy.

Stell. [*to Æonia*]. Tell me 'tis false.

> |[*Æonia remains silent and motionless.*]

                    Tell me, thou treacherous fiend !

Cai.   He needs an answer, chick .... and so do I.

Art thou to be my wife?   Say.

Æon.   We agreed it.

Stellio, forgive me.   'Twas for both our sakes ;

For if so thy life——   .

Stell. [*breaks in*]. Oh gods, to have loved her so !

Æon. kneels, and clings to Stellio.

*Caius laughs boisterously.   A peal of laughter from within is
heard.*

Cai.   They laugh at table too ; but with less cause.

> [*Stellio throws Æonia from him.*

Cai. Hey! Have a care! Mistake her not for Lælia.
Thou'lt hurt my wife, good Stellio.

    Æon. [*to Caius*].   Monster, peace!

    Cai. Wife's tenderness already, chick. That's good.

    Stell. [*to Æonia*]. Thou shalt not do it. Die with me, trait-
ress! Die!   [*Rushes at her. She struggles in terror.*

    Cai. [*gives Æonia a dagger*]. Save thyself. Strike!

                        [*Æonia stabs Stellio.*

    Stell. Oh! Lælia! [*falls motionless.*]

    Cai.   Cleverly struck!
But hast thou killed so quickly? Aye, he's dead.
No more than that? He has passed too easily:
I would have had him taste his dying more.

    Æon. [*stands gazing at Stellio*]. Was it I?

    Cai.   Stand over him so: Yes,
    struck to stone.
Dumb grief at gaze .... a very pretty pose:
We'll draw the curtains back on that. [*calls*] Ho! Some one!
Here, fellows, pull the cords.

    Æon.   Was it I? Was it I?

The curtains are drawn back leaving the banquet hall open again.

    Cai. Come, all of you, come! Another mime! Come quick!

    Æon. Beware!—Stop them!—They'll see it, Caius!

    Cai.   Come, all!

Guests, Children, Actors, Musicians, Servants, Caius's Atten-
dants, etc., all gather round.

    Cai. Now, there's a bridal show! A bleeding bridegroom!

Dead.   And he called on Lælia.   That was good.
Æonia stabbed him ; but she had poisoned him first.

Murmurs and ejaculations of amazement and horror.   Æonia
stands thunderstruck, after a first movement of startled surprise.

Cai.   Hush talk.   I'll tell ye more.   You see her there :
Invincible, was she famed ?   Cold ?   Proudly chaste ?
She was his paramour.

Æon.   'Tis false.

Cai.   For months.

First at Rome, warily ; then, egged on by checks,
Kicking against restraint, they carried their loves
(The baseness of it !) to Baiæ, to Æonia's ;
And Lælia with them—trusting cheated guest !
There closed her in slow snaky coils, till they stung.
They did not kill her, no ; though that they planned :
They found a safer way, drove her to madness,
Set horror and grief to scare her to her death,
Then, having her dead, they thought their secret safe.
But, no.   I, Cæsar, knew.   I heard, saw, sentenced :
And, lo the lovers now !

[A pause.]   Ye stand all scared.

Dares none ask why the wanton killed her mate ?

Marc.   Tell us.   We know not what to ask.

Cai.   Ask *her.*

Quint.   She would not answer it.

Cai.   [*to Æonia*].   Chick, wilt thou tell ?

Font. Poor soul, she's stricken numb. But *she* kill *him!*
That's clear mistake : we know she could not do it.

Cai. To have him silent-safe, Fonteia, she killed him.
I, as Heaven's gods let men achieve their schemes,
Dooming in that success their punishment,
So dealt with these two : each achieved to-day
The hoped success ; he to be wedding her,
And she—what think ye ? [*laughs*] Why, that's her success.
　　　　　　　　　　　　　　　　　　[*Points to Stellio.*

That gives her right of marriage pledge—on whom ?
Rome's sacred head, the Cæsar, the Augustus, Me !

　　　Murmurs and signs of surprise.

1st Guest. That's news indeed !

2nd Guest.　　　　　　　　　　What's meant ?

Others talking confusedly.　　　　What said he ? Marriage ?

Æmil. Caius, could Lælia's murderess be thy wife ?

Cai. Oh, be content, Æmilia ; thou hast vengeance.
[*To the crowd.*] Hush ! Listen, friends. This virtuous-famed
　　Æonia,
Whom now ye know for a greedy light-of-love,
Had passages with me too. She's not stony,
Albeit she look so now ; she had eyes then,
Though it seem not now, for more than only Stellio :
She was mine as much as his.

Æon.　　　　　　　　　Shame ! [*wearily*] All thou wilt.

Cai. She was mine and his. There's beauty there for two ;
And, please it such a woman to please me,
Why, then I'm pleased : for mine's an amorous heart.

And she'd be second Livia, that she would :
So he had three deaths....poison ; then knowing her ;
Then her clever stab.   I could kiss her for it again.

   Æmil.   Is she so vile a thing?   Oh, my poor Lælia !

   Euth.   The blood-stained wanton !   Oh, that she, foul she,
Should canker such a worth as Stellio's was !
H—ss, murderess !

Some of the bystanders join in sounds and shows of execration.

   Quint.   Caius, what's her doom ?

   Some of the bystanders.   Death !   Death !

   Cai.   He tasted *his*—Not long enough, but well.
'Twas good, Æmilia, good !   But *her* doom's slower—
More leisure for the savouring.   An ill goal :
'Tis Pandataria.   Dost thou hear, Æonia ?

   Æon.   Thou wilt not let me die ?

   Cai.   Life will hurt more.

[*Shouts*] Ho !   Lictors !   Jailers !

Enter through curtains in the further part of the banquet hall
                    Lictors, Soldiers, *and* Others.

   Neda.   Lord Caius, send me too.
She was ever kind to me.   She'll need a servant.

   Cai.   I'll grant thee misery if thou ask : think first.
'Tis no free exile in some lesser Rome,
Where life stirs on although the streets be small ;
'Tis prison in a coop of sea-bound rock,
When the jading days have never a change nor hope ;
'Tis, for thy mistress, infamy....thou'lt share.

She'll have hard come-by fare, a beggarly hut,
Where there's no breath for heat in the scorching noons
And the rains break through and the wind screams in the chinks,
And in the winters there's the pinch of cold
Beside the fireless hearth, in threadbare rags——
All that's for her thou'lt need to share.   Dost ask it?
For always, note, for always : no recall :
She'll moulder there to the end....thou, all her while.
Dost ask?

    Neda.   I—No.   Oh, must she suffer all that?

    Cai.   More than that.   More.

    Æon.   More than but that, my Neda :
So those base outward miseries may be help,
Drawing me from the inner some whiles, harshly.
But fret not thou : and leave me with clear heart ;
I need thee not, good girl : I need no kindness.

    Cai.   Neda's thy name ; art she that convoyed me?
She that took Memnon's message?   Thou hast served me :
That ever brings reward.   Neda, thou'rt rich :
I give thee all that was thy mistress's.
No prison, eh? but gold and feasts and Rome.
Espouse her, Memnon.

    Memn.   Thankfully, with that fortune.

    Cai.   It fits well ; since all Stellio had is thine.

    Æmil.   'Tis the children's !   Caius!

    Cai.   Never fear for them.
I'll give them better fortunes, but not his.
Life, and their mother's death, they'll owe to him :

Nought else.

Æmil. Well.

Cai. To the feast ! To the feast, good friends !
Here's bride and bridegroom for us. [*To Memnon and Neda*]
    Come, you two.

—But stay : I swore by myself. Æonia, hark :
I do not break my oath ; I'll wed thee now—
Wed thee and take thee home my very wife.
At day-dawn I'll divorce thee : but what then ?
I shall have been thy bridegroom. Claim my oath.
Wilt thou not, chick ? Come. [*Advances to her.*

Æon. Touch me not, buffoon.

Cai. 'Tis *thy* denial, then. *I*'m very willing.
Come, chick, be Livia to me these next hours.

Æon. Dear Euthymus, kill me. Kill *him* too, for Rome's
    sake.

Cai. Why, if thou wilt not, then my faith is kept.
[*Calls*] Forward there ! Take your prisoner away.

Lictors approach Æonia.

Æon. [*kneels and kisses Stellio's hand gently; then rises
and clasps her hands in agony*]. I loved thee. I *did* love
thee.

Stell. [*murmurs faintly*]. Children—The children.

Cai. Come back again, art thou ? Why, thou lingering fool,
Was not one dying enough ?

Euth. Sir, he has passed.

Cai. Art sure? Stellio, how darest thou name thy children? They are Lælia's. Be thou never so dead, hear *that*.

Æmil. [*leads the children to the dead body*]. Yet kiss him, children, for he was your father.

THE END.

WORKS BY THE SAME AUTHOR

PUBLISHED BY MACMILLAN & CO.

BEDFORD STREET, COVENT GARDEN,

WITH

OPINIONS OF THE PRESS.

—◆—

THE PROMETHEUS BOUND OF ÆSCHYLUS.
Literally translated into English Verse. Extra fcp. 8vo.
3s. 6d.

'Among recent translations of poetry Mrs. Webster's *Prometheus of Æschylus* claims a high rank. Of her volume of original poems we have already spoken. Her translation is marked by the same high qualities, but especially by fidelity to the original without losing its spirit.'—*Westminster Review*.

'It has clearly been a labour of love, and has been done faithfully and conscientiously.'—*Contemporary Review*.

'We have been often quite amazed at the extent to which she has complied with the severe conditions imposed on herself.'—*Nonconformist*.

'The translation may be regarded in its entirety as a really marvellous performance ; it is astonishing how a certain poetic majesty, for which the original is remarkable, discloses itself in the choral portions and the monologues. . . . The scholar will acknowledge the difficulty of the task undertaken, and will be struck with no infrequent surprise and admiration at the art and ingenuity with which troublesome passages are handled.'—*Illustrated London News*.

DRAMATIC STUDIES.

Extra fcp. 8vo. 5s.

'A volume marked by many signs of remarkable power.'—*Saturday Review.*

'Mrs. Webster shows not only originality, but, what is nearly as rare, trained intellect and self-command. She possesses, too, what is the first requisite of a poet—earnestness. This quality is stamped upon all that she writes.'—*Westminster Review.*

'A volume as strongly marked by perfect taste as by poetic power.'—*Nonconformist.*

'Expositions of separate individualities profoundly studied and minutely realised.'—*Athenæum.*

A WOMAN SOLD, and other Poems.

Extra fcp. 8vo. 7s. 6d.

'In many places, too, we have glimpses of an admirably subtle analytic power.'—*Saturday Review.*

'Enough has been cited to show that the writer has the vision which looks not only deeply into the heart, but lovingly upon nature.'—*Athenæum.*

'Mrs. Webster has shown us that she is able to draw admirably from the life ; that she can observe with subtlety, and render her observations with delicacy ; that she can impersonate complex conceptions, and venture into recesses of the ideal world into which few living writers can follow her.'—*Guardian.*

THE MEDEA OF EURIPIDES.

Literally translated into English verse. Extra fcp. 8vo. 3s. 6d.

'The *Medea* has hitherto had many imitators, but few English translators, and none who have performed the work with as much honesty and general ability as Mrs. Webster.'—*Pall Mall Gazette.*

' It is surprising how closely and correctly she has repro-
duced the original, expressing its full force and delicate shades
of meaning line for line, and almost word for word.'—
Athenæum.

' We really do not know where to find another translation
in which the spirit is rendered with such fidelity and beauty.'—
Westminster Review.

PORTRAITS.

Fcp. 8vo. 3*s*. 6*d*.

' We have been more than liberal in our quotations from
these gems because it is so seldom that one now meets with what
is really poetry in the highest sense of the term.   It is long
since we encountered a volume of short miscellaneous pieces
which would bear reading a second time.   Many of those now
before us, however, can be perused again and again with in-
creasing pleasure.   Whole lines cling to the memory as only
the " winged words " of genius can do, and refuse to be cast out
of the chambers of the brain."—*Examiner.*

' Here we must stop.   We feel that we have not done the
poem justice.   Nor will our readers, we fear, be able to judge
of its beauties by our extracts.   The poem must be read like
the others in the book—as a whole.   Lastly, we do not expect
Mrs. Webster to be popular all at once ; but if she only remains
true to herself she will most assuredly take a higher rank as a
poet than any woman has yet done.'—*Westminster Review.*

THE AUSPICIOUS DAY.

Extra fcp. 8vo. 5*s*.

' In our opinion *The Auspicious Day* shows a marked
advance, not only in art, but, what is of far more importance,
in breadth of thought and intellectual grasp.'—*Westminster
Review.*

' It is quite impossible by extracts to convey any true idea

of the remarkable strength and subtlety of this drama.   Like
all true dramatic products it has a verisimilitude which does not
show well in separate passages ; but let any person of the least
susceptibility read the trial scene, and . . . . we are sure that
his verdict will be ours—that for simplicity, naturalness, and
pathetic effect, he has seldom read anything finer.'—*Nonconformist.*

 ' There is a dramatic severity and strength throughout—
evidence of a sustained and lofty creative instinct—which should
be sufficient to deepen and extend Mrs. Webster's already well-
won poetic reputation.   We should not forget to say that the
songs scattered throughout the poem are clear, vivid, and con-
densed, as only true lyrics are ; and that we have snatches of
racy, unaffected humour, the best proof and fruit of real
dramatic faculty.'—*British Quarterly Review.*

YU-PE-YA'S LUTE.

 A Chinese Tale in English Verse.   Extra fcp. 8vo. 3*s.* 6*d.*
 ' Mrs. Webster here adds another proof to many she has
previously given, as it has been our pleasure to note, of her
title to a high, if peculiar, place in the rich roll of our living
poets.'—*Scotsman.*

 ' *Yu-Pe-Ya's Lute* is slight, but is graceful and attractive.
The versification is very smooth and sweet, and several of the
songs—especially "Waiting, waiting" are beautiful. . . . .
Yu-Pe-Ya's Lute achieves a success which is denied to many
more pretentious efforts.   It is a quaint and pleasing trifle ;
all the more attractive that it affords at least a glimpse into a
life and literature which, to most English readers, is as strange
as that of another planet.'—*Times.*

 ' The poem is knit close in the strain of noble ideas, is
sweetly simple in flow of narrative, rising now and then into
fine dramatic passages.   The occasional mixture of artificial
phrase, no doubt derived from the original, with a quaint sim-

plicity which is the author's own, often intensifies the pathos of the piece.   No extracts could do justice to it.'—*Nonconformist.*

'We close the book with a renewed conviction that in Mrs. Webster we have a profound and original poet.   *Yu-Pe-Ya's Lute* is marked not by mere sweetness of melody—rare as that gift is—but by the infinitely rarer gifts of dramatic power, of passion, and of sympathetic insight.'—*Westminster Review.*

A HOUSEWIFE'S OPINIONS.
Crown 8vo. 7s. 6d.

'We have seldom met with so much common sense and honest mother-wit in a small compass.   It is a selection of short treatises, for the most part on social or domestic subjects, abounding in true womanly insight, and in penetrating and often profound criticisms, which are wanting neither in sympathy nor in severity.'—*Daily News.*

'No one can read Mrs. Webster's books without immediately perceiving that she is a woman of genius, possessed of remarkable common sense and a rare facility of expression.   Her translations from the Greek are among the very best we possess, and her *Dramatic Studies* is a very original and vigorous book.   Now she wins once more deserved and universal praise for a work which, if it be not altogether to our old-fashioned taste, is full of sound reasoning, and well merits to be carefully studied.'—*Morning Post.*

'Mrs. Webster has gathered together a number of her essays on common every-day subjects.   They show a remarkable versatility of power in the translator of Greek dramatists and the author of original poetical works of great beauty.   She descends as easily as she rises, and if the admirable critique on Browning's translation of Æschylus's *Agamemnon*, which appears in her volume, seems thrown in to prove it is the same Augusta Webster who has often charmed us in works of imagination, we can have no doubt it is a very practical lady whose opinions range over topics such as are here discussed.'—*Leeds Mercury.*

'For the most part light in style, and pervaded by a humour as keen as it is bright, these papers are nevertheless full of solid thought, truthful observation, and practical wisdom. Questions of social economy and of public morals, æsthetic, educational, and literary topics, are handled with refreshing breadth of view, with abundant knowledge, and with a literary grace and vigour such as might have been anticipated from the accomplished writer.'—*Scotsman.*

A BOOK OF RHYME.

Extra fcp. 8vo. 3*s*. 6*d*.

'An interesting portion of this volume consists of beautiful little rural poems, which the author calls " English *Stornelli*." . . . . Her readers are indebted to her for reproducing in our own language a form of popular poetry which is more delightful than any other in Europe.'—*Athenæum.*

'She chooses in some instances a very common theme ; but she never fails, by a few graceful and unexpected touches, to redeem it from commonplaceness, and often to impart to it an elevation, dignity, and suggestiveness peculiar to herself.'—*Nonconformist.*

'In profundity, grasp, and boldness of thought, in acute insight into the intricacies of human nature, in grandeur of conception and skill in embodying her ideas in worthy forms, the author need fear comparison with few living poets.'—*Scotsman.*

'Though it has by verse of a different, that is, of a stronger quality than what we have, for the most part, in this volume that Mrs. Webster achieved her high level among living poets, even this is what few of her rivals could match.'—*Spectator.*

'Mrs. Webster is a sweet and graceful singer. All her work, whether it be poetry or prose, drama or translation, bears on it the stamp and impression of a strong and thoughtful intel-

lect allied to a vivid power of artistic representation.   It was to
be expected, therefore, that *A Book of Rhyme* would contain
poems of a higher order than the modest title suggests, and the
expectation was not formed in vain. . . . . The *Stornelli* are a
series of wonderful picture verses, *huitains*, containing each a
little study, carved like a gem by a skilful master-hand.'—
Westminster Review.

_____

PUBLISHED BY C. KEGAN PAUL & CO.

1 PATERNOSTER SQUARE.

DISGUISES.

Extra fcp. 8vo. 5*s.*

'The reason why poets of Mrs. Webster's rank write dramas
is very obvious—because here only can they find real scope for
their genius.   In a five-act play they are able, if we may use
so strong an expression, to give vent to their feelings and pas-
sions under the mask of impersonality.   They can also give to
the world, by means of their characters, their own views on
social questions, no less than on religion, and this, too, in the
most effective manner.   The five-act play too admits of many
measures.   It sails not with one sail.   Above all here can the
artist indulge in the artist's true delight—that of drawing characters.   For these reasons poets like Mrs. Webster find in the
five-act drama the only channel into which they can freely pour
their thoughts. . . . Whether the intellectual classes might be
won back [*i.e.*, to the theatre] by such writers as Tennyson and
Mrs. Webster if they adapt themselves to new forms of art is
the problem. . . . Above all things lyrical poetry is Mrs.
Webster's strong point.   Here, for instance, is a delightful song,
etc., which borrows nothing from the Elizabethan dramatists,
but is essentially modern in feeling. . . . We should have liked
to have given some passages showing Mrs. Webster's dramatic
power and insight into human nature.'—*Westminster Review.*

'The whole character and construction of this drama assign it to a type with which a very powerful tone of emotion would not accord, and in avoiding this Mrs. Webster has shown artistic self-restraint. It belongs in fact to the class of romantic dramas of which *As You Like It* is one of the finest, and *Love's Labour Lost* one of the purest examples. Even by its fresh woodland scenery, and the glad open-air breeze which blows about its pages, it reminds us of those famous scenes in the forests of Ardennes and of Navarre; and the piquant contrast of peasant and courtier recalls the more brilliant scenes in which Audrey serves for foil to Touchstone, and the country simplicity of Colin sets in rich relief the courtly wit of Rosalind. No doubt the genius of the nineteenth century comes out in Mrs. Webster's drawing of her Republican peasants, who appear fully the equals of their visitors, both in wit and manners, and by much their superiors in honesty. Shakespeare nowhere shows any trace of this thoroughly modern point of view. Where his subject led him nearest to it, etc., etc. . . . But it is not merely by the buoyant outdoor air, nor by the piquant contrast of courtiers and peasants, that *Disguises* suggests the manner of the Romantic Drama. A construction somewhat loose and free; interest diffused among several groups, instead of being concentrated upon some Hamlet or Macbeth; a plot full of surprises, rapid changes, sharp oppositions, and pervaded by a certain delicate air of artificiality or even caprice, which gives the impression that it is the mere charm of variety as much as any deeper law which determines its movements; characters, finally, not of the heroic mould which retains its purposes with unrelaxing grip to the end, but of a type in which this grim strength of the Puritan passes into the more flexible and versatile nature of Southern Europe; such are the broad features of the Romantic Drama, and of these there is not a little in Mrs. Webster's book. . . . Then, again, that tragic intensity which would have accorded as ill with the checkered but nowhere profound shadows of the Romantic Drama as a harsh war-trumpet breaking upon a pastoral symphony of lutes and lyres, is carefully avoided.'—*Spectator.*

'Mrs. Webster has the true dramatic instinct. . . . Her dialogue is managed with the utmost art ; she knows precisely where to stop in view of her immediate purpose. . . . Gual-hardine, the lovely grandchild of the chief magistrate of the little rustic Republic of St. Fabien in Aquitaine, is most daintily con-ceived. . . . Some of the songs sprinkled through the scenes are exceedingly fine.'—*British Quarterly Review.*

'To say that *Disguises* can be read a second time with more pleasure than the first is a just tribute to the literary ability of its author, who has already gained an honourable place among present writers. . . . Its good bits could be picked out by hundreds.'—*Academy.*

'The dialogue is always excellent, pure, and beautiful, so far as English is concerned—simple always, sometimes quaint, and full of lines that ought to be remembered. The little songs scattered through the play are very beautiful.'—*Nonconformist.*

'Mrs. Webster, whose fitness for such an undertaking is foreshadowed in her *Dramatic Studies*, and in her noble trans-lations of the *Prometheus Bound* and *Medea*, has produced an original drama which is by far the most important contribution made to this department of English literature in recent years. Whether *Disguises* would be a stage success is a question that could only be decided by actual experience. Very likely it would not, for Mrs. Webster's method is not that of the prac-tised playwright, who writes "up" to an effective tableau, and knows how to tickle the ears of the groundlings. Moreover, there is scarcely one of the characters in this drama that would not require conscientious and intelligent study in order to grasp its full scope, and real histrionic ability to convey its true significance to an audience. Again, the dramatic feeling by which the work is pervaded, intense and true though it be, does not find ex-pression in those broad and highly-coloured forms which are most telling upon the stage. Nevertheless, it is hard to believe

that a play so full of charm, of poetic grace, of the subtle ana-
lysis and forcible contrast of different character-types, would,
if adequately represented, fail to interest and please ; and if Mr.
Irving is in want of a really good original play by an English
writer, he might do worse than turn his attention to this of Mrs·
Webster's.   It is, at any rate, delightful to read.   To attempt
a description of the plot would be to spoil it.   The scene is
laid in sunny Aquitaine ; the time is that when the spirit of
chivalry was still dominant ; the theme is the triumph of the
love of a true and high-minded man and a pure and noble-
hearted woman over the intrigues of political ambition and the
pride of race.   The personages are powerfully conceived and
consistently wrought out, while the action is natural and skil-
fully sustained, and the dialogue combines poetical force and
beauty with dramatic effect in a very exceptional degree.'—
Scotsman.

IN A DAY.

Extra fcp. 8vo.   2s. 6d.

' The volume can hardly fail to increase Mrs. Webster's reputation as a Dramatist.'—*Athenæum.*

' There is something fine in the conception of Klydone's
death, and with suitable actors the play would be effective on
the stage.'—*Morning Post.*

' Mrs. Webster's subject in this case is hardly such as would
please the mass of readers ; but she has worked out the play
with admirable art and some of the speeches are instinct with
dramatic truth, and here and there we have touches of pathos
that are more effective from the severe self-restraint of the style.'
—*Nonconformist.*

' Whatever Mrs. Webster's pen finds to write is written with
rare grace and considerable power.   For her new drama " In a
Day " we have little but words of praise, and we regret that the
space at our disposal will not allow us to do full justice to so
delicate a work of art.'—*Westminster Review.*

www.ingramcontent.com/pod-product-compliance
Lightning Source LLC
Chambersburg PA
CBHW020236030726
47497CB00009B/3120